CHILDREN OF THE VOLCANO

Other Books from LAWRENCE HILL on Central America and the Caribbean

Jamaica Under Manley
Dilemmas of Socialism and Democracy
Michael Kaufman

Bitter Grounds — 2nd Edition
Roots of Revolt in El Salvador
Liisa North

ALISON ACKER

CHILDREN OF THE VOLCANO

between the lines

LAWRENCE HILL & CO.
520 RIVERSIDE AVE., WESTPORT, CONNECTICUT 06880

© 1986 Between The Lines

Published by Between The Lines,
        229 College Street,
        Toronto, Ontario M5T 1R4
        Lawrence Hill & Co.
        520 Riverside Ave.
        Westport, Connecticut

Photographs by Alison Acker
Typeset by Canadian Composition
Cover design by Goodness Graphics

Cover illustration courtesy of the Central American Refugee Children's Drawings Project, sponsored by Inter-Pares and CUSO, Ottawa.

Cover drawing is by Ovidio, an eleven-year-old displaced Salvadorean.

Between The Lines receives financial assistance from the Canada Council and the Ontario Arts Council.

Between The Lines is a joint project of Dumont Press Graphix, Kitchener, and the Development Education Centre, Toronto.

Canadian Cataloguing in Publication Data
Acker, Alison, 1928-
    Children of the volcano

ISBN 0-919946-66-6 (bound) 0-919946-67-4 (pbk.)

1. Children — Central America. 2. Youth — Central America.
3. Central America — Politics and government — 1979-
4. Central America — Economic conditions — 1979-
5. Central America — Social conditions — 1979-   . I. Title.

HQ792.C35A35 1986   305.2'3'09728   C86-093593-0

*To my sons, who are lucky, and to Harold,
whose memory went with me every step
of the way.*

Table of Contents

PREFACE

IN 1984 I went to Central America. My trip was not a diplomatic jetting between capitals to talk with experts, nor was it to spend time working with the poor as a member of a work brigade or charity. I travelled unescorted, equipped only with a tape recorder and an intense curiosity, to the capitals, small villages, and refugee camps of the area in order to find out what life is like for the many children and youth who live with poverty and war. I spent four months travelling and interviewing children and teenagers in Guatemala, El Salvador, Honduras, and Nicaragua. *Children of the Volcano* is the result.

This is not a scientific survey. I did not deliberately choose a statistically-accurate sampling of rich children, poor children, or refugee children. Rather, I simply interviewed people I met on my travels. For the most part they represent victims of violence, those trying to improve their lot, and those trying to help others. Readers will find very few kids in this book whom we in the West regard as "average" or "normal" — the Pepsi generation in their designer jeans — because those kids are not typical or even visible in Central America. In fact, how the youth of Central America spend their lives challenges all our usual concepts of proper childhood.

All the interviews were conducted in private, in Spanish, and using verbatim shorthand, since I was quickly made aware that tape recorders are viewed with suspicion. The youngest I interviewed was seven, the oldest twenty-four. Some could barely tell their stories; others showed an amazing ability to express and analyse their experiences. All of them opened my eyes to the riches that they have to offer in spite of their youth, in spite of their circumstances. I have used a pseudonym in only one interview, but in others I have not used the full name for fear of retribution.

Some interviews arose by chance; others were arranged through official channels or through humanitarian, church, development, or clandestine groups. It is impossible to thank all these sources adequately for their help, and it would be dangerous to mention many of them by name.

I would like to thank Donna Fine for her encouragement during the first drafting of this book, and Dinah Forbes for her patient and perceptive editing.

I know there are many more terrible and inspiring stories that are waiting to be told. The children and youth of Central America who live the days of their lives under the volcanic pressures of poverty, repression, and revolution will, some day, be able to speak for themselves. It would be presumptuous of me to thank the children who told me their stories, as I am only an intermediary. This is, after all, their book.

A.A., January 1986

INTRODUCTION

THERE ARE eleven million children and teenagers in Guatemala, El Salvador, Honduras, and Nicaragua. Children outnumber adults almost three to one. But this book is not a story of too many children, rather it is a story of child neglect and abuse; a story of a war against the innocent, of *people* struggling to satisfy basic needs.

In Central America many, many children are born sick and die hungry. They do not play. Their guns are often real guns, their chores are day-long labour, and their dreams are nightmares of killing. Most of their governments ignore them, reject them, or maltreat them. They have inherited centuries of exploitation and injustice, and now they are victims of war.

Children have been the pawns of the mighty ever since Herod slaughtered the Innocents. During the past fifty years, children have been slaughtered in Auschwitz, Hiroshima, Lebanon, Uganda, Indonesia, Biafra, Chile, Vietnam, Cambodia, Argentina, Ireland — the list goes on. The enormity of their suffering appalls us, yet deadens us. Their distance from our comfortable homes relieves us. What is new is the closeness of the Central America conflict to the North American consciousness — and conscience. Ninety minutes' flying time from Miami, soldiers are raping children.

Once upon a time, the "banana republics" of Central America

could be dismissed and even their massacres ignored. Now we have made them part of superpower politics. What happens there explodes on Western TV screens as Vietnam once did, but this time it is happening in North America's backyard. The kids who fled to refugee camps in Mexico and Honduras were the first to capture public attention. But for every child in a refugee camp, hundreds suffer poverty and war in their own countries. Outsiders want to help them, but help is made difficult by world politics. It is difficult and dangerous for aid organizations to operate in countries like Guatemala, where human rights organizations such as Amnesty International are refused entry. Local people working for the disadvantaged disappear regularly. Aid money is diverted by corrupt officials or used to whitewash unsavoury regimes and legitimize them in the eyes of the world. In Central America even church aid may be put to political use.

In the confused cauldron of Central American politics, it is no wonder that kind-hearted donors are fearful their aid might go to "the wrong side," whichever side that might be. And so the children suffer.

They have been suffering for centuries. Violence against the poor began with the Spanish conquest of Central America five hundred years ago. The Indian population was decimated by massacres, overwork, and disease. The start of export agriculture (coffee, cotton, sugar, and bananas) and some industry made only a few families and transnational companies rich: the poor stayed poor. Those who rebelled against forced labour or tried to organize for a better life were jailed, tortured, exiled, or killed. Since 1900, the gap between the rich and the poor has widened steadily, in spite of economic aid from the United States.

In the 1950s, the first real attempt at land reform was made in Guatemala. Snuffed out when it threatened the plantations of the United Fruit Company, the attempt was seen as a "communist threat" by the U.S. government. Since then, Guatemala has suffered a series of military regimes that have waged war against the Indian peasant population in a vain attempt to root out sympathy for a small band of guerrillas. The country is now a nation of "protected villages," reminiscent of the Vietnam war, where "pacified" peasants depend upon the army for their survival.

Civil war has been raging in El Salvador since 1979. The country is split: the eastern third has been won by FDR/FMLN rebels, who have their own form of popular government,[1] the western third is in government control, the rest is in dispute. Death squads routinely leave corpses in the gutters, but it is the bombing of civilians by government forces that causes the most deaths. Children die from bullets, bombs, and napalm burns. Thousands are homeless or orphaned.

In Honduras, it is poverty that kills the children. The country shares with Bolivia the "honour" of being the most impoverished nation in Latin America. The coming of U.S. military aid and military bases has neither improved the economy nor helped share out what little wealth the country possesses. Counterrevolutionaries using Honduran bases to make war on Nicaragua compound Honduras's problems still further, and make its neutrality in the Central American conflict impossible.

In Nicaragua, Anastasio Somoza's dictatorship fell in 1979, bringing the victory of the Sandinista revolution. Although the Sandinistas have formed a pluralistic government, which not only allows private enterprise but largely depends upon it, Nicaragua continues to be boycotted, harassed, and attacked by the U.S. government. The Reagan administration aids the counterrevolutionaries, known as the "contras," in their attacks on Nicaragua from neighbouring Honduras and Costa Rica. Thousands of Nicaraguans, including many teenagers who volunteered for defence duty, have been killed as a result. The attacks and the prolonged militarization of Nicaragua have also weakened a shaky economy and held up health and welfare programs.

Since 1979, at least a hundred and fifty thousand people have been killed by the violence in Central America; many have been children. But war and poverty have killed other children more slowly, through malnutrition or through childhood diseases that could have been prevented by properly-funded health programs. Despite UNICEF programs to encourage rehydration and vaccination, infant mortality in the region remains eight times that of Canada or the United States.[2] Increased military budgets

---

[1] FDR/FMLN. Formed in 1980, the Democratic Revolutionary Front (FDR) and the Farabundo Martí National Liberation Front (FMLN) brought together, for the first time, the revolutionary opposition in El Salvador into one body.

[2] The United Nations International Children's Emergency Fund (UNICEF) was formed in 1946 and currently operates in 112 countries. Its funding comes

Home is a cardboard box for this typical street child in Tegucigalpa, Honduras.

have brought cuts in health and education spending, so that instead of building hospitals and schools, Central America's regimes are closing them down. After the army's needs have been seen to, there is no money left to pay nurses, doctors, and teachers. Add to this the rising price for basic food and the fall in average incomes since 1979, and it is easy to see why the children die or never reach their potential.

Foreigners make understandable errors when they guess a Central American kid's age. They are, indeed, small for their age because they live on tortillas (corn pancakes), if they can get them, and sometimes a few beans. That's all. It is a diet deficient in protein, vitamins, and calories, and it stunts mental and physical growth.

The war in Central America has an emotional effect, too. Children who have watched their parents murdered, who have been raped or tortured themselves, children who have been orphaned, abandoned, imprisoned, and beaten, may well have been damaged for life. There is no one officially measuring the

from voluntary sources and its work depends on local government support.

trauma, much less attempting to heal the traumatized, only a dedicated few who battle official indifference.

It is remarkable how few studies there have been of children from other wars. There is scant information on the children of the concentration camps in Germany and Poland, on the Vietnam boat people's kids, on the children of the disappeared people of Chile and Argentina. The few studies attempted have reached only tentative conclusions: yes, recovery is easier if a child has the security of family and easier for the young children than for the pre-adolescent or adolescent child. But nobody is sure why some children stay whole and others go under. And no psychiatrist has ever been to that church basement in San Salvador, where refugee children spend their days, or to that "widows' village" in Guatemala, where every child is fatherless.

The children in Honduran refugee camps have externalized something of their anguish in drawings. Their pictures show bombs falling like rain. They draw stick figures of mothers and fathers lying flat, with a leg missing or a head chopped off. The men with guns have fangs like animals. But other kids have never had pencil and paper, and they have learned from infancy to suffer in silence.

The miracle is that so many of them survive and flourish, and that they have so little hate. Not one of the children or teenagers I interviewed for this book mentioned desire for revenge, either against an individual or against the society that had treated them so badly. Instead, they were concerned about their parents, or about smaller brothers or sisters. They felt responsible for helping out, either by bringing in money or doing chores. They yearned for simple things like an orange or shoes. They dreamed of being spacemen or of getting married.

Very few of the teenagers approved of or enjoyed violence, even those carrying guns. They were surprisingly mild in spite of the terrors they lived in and the warlike propaganda that surrounded them. Many showed amazing courage when confronting adults who held power of life or death over them. Some deliberately risked their lives to help the poor and weak. The children in this book are not just victims; many of them are actively trying to change their own lives and those of others, in societies where this attempt is dangerous.

The waste of such children and young people is more serious, even, than the individual suffering. In El Salvador, Guatemala, and Honduras, to be young is to be suspected of being subversive. To be a child means being unwanted, useless. In Nicaragua, the young are privileged, but privilege has brought with it an enormous burden of duty to society, even to the point of sacrificing one's life.

To be young in Central America is so different from Western concepts of what childhood should be. The fun, play, and imaginative experiences we feel are an essential part of growing up cannot be taken for granted: often they are missing entirely. French novelist Jacques Danois, who visited the children of Cambodia, has commented: "The sick child can be cared for and fed but no one has invented a replacement for childhood."[3]

In 1969, the General Assembly of the United Nations unanimously adopted the Declaration of the Rights of the Child. Its preamble states that "mankind owes the child the best it has to give." It insists that the child is entitled to special protection and opportunities, education, food, housing, recreation, and medical services. Finally, it asserts that the child shall be brought up "in a spirit of understanding, tolerance, friendship among peoples, peace and universal brotherhood, in full consciousness that his energy and talents should be devoted to the service of his fellow men."

The child whose home is a cardboard box one street from a luxury hotel where generals and politicians meet and plan how to spend millions on munitions might wonder at our duplicity. Albert Einstein put our dilemma very succinctly:

"There are no great discoveries or great progress so long as there is an unhappy child on the earth."[4]

[3] Jacques Danois, "Children of the Fire," *UNICEF News*, 1980, issue 106.
[4] Albert Einstein, *Ideas and Opinions of Albert Einstein* (New York: Crown Publishing, 1954).

Part One

GUATEMALA

GUATEMALA CITY has the sharp, thin smell of fear. The beggars are silent. The fruit vendors are hushed. School children walk quietly, all eyes on the police armed with sub-machine guns and on the army trucks prowling the streets. Outside the bus terminal a man sprawls face down on the sidewalk. The crowds step over him. Drunk or dead? Don't ask in Guatemala. Ragged kids pick over the rotten fruit in the gutter beside him.

Statistics cannot convey Guatemala's sadness adequately. The horror of military rule collides with the beauty and the history of its victims.

Once upon a time the Mayans lived in peace, in terraced cities of stone surrounded by an emerald jungle where parrots flew and jaguars stalked. They knew astronomy and a thousand years ago created calendars more accurate than ours. They carved and wrote poetry, farmed, and traded. And then the Spaniards came.

"They came and undid everything. They taught fear. They withered the flowers. They came only to castrate the sun. And their children stayed with us and we receive only their bitterness," wrote the Mayan sage Chilam Balam, nearly five hundred years ago.[5]

The armed men who once rode on horseback now ride tanks.

[5] *The Book of Chilam Balam of Chumayel*, translated by Ralph L. Roys (Hagerstown, Maryland: University of Oklahoma Press, 1967).

The Guatemalan army controls the government, industry and agriculture, law, schools, roads, banks, the press, and the minds of Guatemalans. Since 1954, when the military came to power, news of Guatemala's violations of human rights has sickened the world.

Maybe one would not care so much if Guatemala was not so beautiful — a land of waterfalls, volcanos, and hot springs — and the Guatemalan people even lovelier. Peasant women with bone-crushing loads on their heads walk like princesses, their skirts swaying in a riot of woven colour. Peasant men in thread-bare jackets and bare, calloused feet greet you with dignity. Their *"adiós"* doesn't mean "good-bye," but is really a prayer, "God be with you," for they are religious people, their beliefs a mingling of faith in the saints, the Virgin Mary, and the Mayan gods of the rain, the corn, and the sun.

More than half the population is pure Indian, the rest a mixture of Spanish and Indian known in Central America as the ladino. The ugliness of the rich ladinos stands out. Society women in beehive hair-dos and too-tight dresses welcome square-headed generals to the opening of yet another glittering government showcase, such as the empty Ministry of Justice.

Four years before, I had left Guatemala City in a hurry, after seventeen of my contacts at the National Workers Central union confederation had been kidnapped, and a man in a jeep without a licence-plate had called out to me and taken my photograph outside the ruined union office. Now, officials tell me, I will notice improvements. Elected representatives are busy writing a constitution. The civilian government elected in 1985 is the first in thirty years. And it is true there are changes, but none for the better.

On my last visit, I counted twenty-four soldiers on the roof of the Presidential Palace, the headquarters of army intelligence. Now there are TV cameras instead that swivel to cover the surrounding streets and sidewalks. Repression has become state-of-the-art.

It began, of course, with the Spaniards, who in a hundred years killed off two-thirds of the Indian population by disease and over-work as well as by the sword. Then came the coffee barons and the banana companies who instituted exploitation. A nine-year reform period, from 1945 to 1954, allowed union organization, freedom of the press, and land reform. The policies culminated in President Jacobo Arbenz's expropriation of the United Fruit Company's unused land.

In response, the United States promptly engineered a mercenary invasion from Honduras and sent planes to bomb Guatemala City. Arbenz resigned and the repression returned, this time with the assistance of the U.S. government. Each turn of the screw led to worker and student protests, protests that turned into popular armed resistance after the Cuban Revolution. U.S. military advisers responded with the co-ordinated counterinsurgency methods they had first practised in Vietnam. During Colonel Carlos Arana Osorio's presidency, between 1970 and 1974, fifteen thousand people were killed in campaigns designed to put down a few hundred guerrillas.

The 1976 earthquake brought international attention to Guatemala. It also provided a shocking education as relief workers discovered the twenty-five thousand dead were almost all poor, killed in the collapse of adobe houses. The rich, in their well-built houses, survived and profited. The Guatemalan newspaper *Impacto* claimed that twenty-seven businessmen rapidly became millionaires through land purchases and building material speculation after the earthquake. In the face of official indifference and corruption, the opposition gathered strength again. Industrial workers formed a broad front, the CNUS (National Committee of Labour Unity). State employees went on strike, and miners and sugar workers marched on the capital.

In 1978, General Romeo Lucas García began a reign of terror, during which eight thousand people died in four years. At Panzos, 108 peasants protesting the theft of their land were massacred. In 1980, peasants occupied the Spanish Embassy in Guatemala City to deliver a protest about human rights violations. They were burned to death after troops stormed the building and threw fire bombs through the windows. Only the Spanish ambassador escaped unharmed. One peasant lived, but was murdered later while lying in his hospital bed.

In 1982, another General, Efraín Ríos Montt, a born-again fundamentalist, took over with a new brand of repression. His government forced thousands of peasants, through starvation and terror, to surrender to the army. The peasants were confined in "model villages" and fed and controlled through a "bullets or beans" program. "If you are with us, we'll feed you; if not, we'll shoot you," was how one army officer put it. U.S., Israeli, and Argentinian aid backed a sophisticated campaign to cut off support and sympathy for the guerrilla bands and to control every hamlet. Another four thousand died in 1982 alone, while supplies worth millions of dollars from the United States reached Ríos Montt's Church of the Word in a program called "International Lovelift."

By 1983, Ríos Montt's excesses under the guise of evangelism had become an embarrassment to the United States. Covertly, the U.S. government engineered another coup, one that placed a new face in control and so allowed a resumption of U.S. military aid. General Oscar Mejía Víctores continued the repression but, at the same time, he courted greater world acceptance of the Guatemalan regime by promising a return to democracy and presidential elections in November 1985. In November, Vinicio Cerezo Arévalo and his Christian Democrat Party won the election, but the army retained effective control of the country, especially in the countryside.

Throughout 1984 and 1985, assassinations continued in the cities and massacres in the countryside, though most peasants were now "contained" in the "pacified" regions. Hunger, unemployment, disease, and food prices were growing worse. There were over one million displaced persons inside the country — one person in every seven — and thousands outside the refugee camps. And I had come to Guatemala to ask about children. There was no child welfare office, no child protection agency, no International Red Cross, no UNICEF, no human rights organization, no progressive church except for a few brave priests. Nobody spoke for the children.

On October 11, 1984, the Guatemalan newspaper *El Día* reported that eight hundred women, most of them under eighteen, had been raped by troops of the Chichicastenango garrison in two months alone. The report was prepared by the Civil Affairs Committee of the Armed Forces.

When I went to see Colonel Héctor Rosales Salavarría, the army's public relations chief, he kept me waiting five hours and then apologized profusely in Texan English for keeping a "lady" waiting. He was sure the *El Día* report had been a mistake.

"We are not like the Communists. We love our children and

Carlos, 15, an Indian boy training to become a rural teacher.

we respect our women." He patted my arm.

Swallowing my anger, I asked for the safe-conduct letter that would introduce me to military commanders in El Quiché province, a two-day bus ride to the north-west. The commanders, he said, would be delighted to show me round. Such a pity that the rains made it impossible for me to get around on my own.

I boarded the bus determined to ignore his veiled warning. But after getting off the bus seven times for an identity check at military check-points, I began to think that Colonel Rosales's letter was indeed working so well that the whole army was expecting me.

Mash

His name is Mash, the Ixil Indian version of Tomás, and he used to be a Guatemalan guerrilla. He's seven or maybe eight years old, nobody knows for sure because Mash isn't saying. He won't say anything. He's been told not to talk.

I found Mash polishing the major's boots in the barracks at Nebaj, a bleak, dirt-road town in the Quiché mountains, for years the centre of conflict between guerrillas and the Guatemalan army and most recently the scene of peasant massacres to wipe out rebel support.

Major Rudolfo Flores pats the boy's head. "Mash is our mascot. Used to be a terrorist." I blink. The kid in the over-sized army T-shirt stares at the major, his eyes black stones. Then he turns and slides away.

Major Flores does not want to talk about Mash. He wants to show off statistics about the army's model villages, where the "beans or bullets" campaign has regrouped displaced peasants under military control. I need the major's permission to visit the camps, but I have to wait for him to decide. And so, to pass the time, I talk to the soldiers, who are evidently fond of the boy but totally indifferent to the horrors of his situation.

"Tough kid, our Mash. His mother and father must have been among those killed in a shoot-out we had last April. Somebody said he had a grenade when he was grabbed and brought in for interrogation. He was kicking and biting, that's for sure. He's been around here now for five months."

"What did he tell you?" I ask.

"Not one word. My guess is that his parents told him not to talk and so he won't say anything at all, though he's not deaf and dumb. He understands Ixil and some Spanish. He won't even tell you his name. He just looks at you with those cold eyes.

"He's smart, though. We discovered he can load a gun faster than any of us, and he knows how to use it, too."

At the Catholic mission up the street the Sister confirms the story. She tells me that the soldiers killed Mash's parents in April and took him in for interrogation.

"They're not bad to him. In fact, they're quite fond of him, especially the major. He's a bit like a mascot. But it's no place for a kid, is it?"

She has no place to keep Mash, and doesn't want trouble with the army. But maybe, she suggests, I can do something. Next day, I go back to the barracks, but I have no plans for Mash, only a helpless concern. By chance, a U.S. doctor is in Major Flores's office, and, like an improbable angel, he is the ideal person to help me rescue Mash. Dr. Carl Heinlein is the sort of cussed American who ignores authority and gets away with it. He also has a clinic in a nearby village, and a children's home called Living Water near Guatemala City. Even more miraculously, the major is slightly drunk and very emotional.

"Take him tomorrow, before I change my mind. I'm not running a boys' home. He'll be ready at eleven a.m."

But at eleven Mash isn't ready. He is hiding. The soldiers have to drag him out of the barracks to our station-wagon and stuff him in the back, where a fellow passenger holds him tight to his chest, arms crossed. Mash still tries to bite. The major appears to wave goodbye, his eyes watering. Another soldier rushes up with Mash's baseball cap and his football.

For seven hours we drive along roads as rough as riverbeds. The boy is stiff, his teeth set, his eyes expressionless. He won't drink a Coke or eat peanuts or a banana when we stop in the market at Santa Cruz del Quiché, the provincial capital. He won't get out of the station-wagon when we finally reach the Living Water home sixteen kilometres west of Guatemala City late that night. We wake up a kid who speaks Ixil to entice him out, but Mash won't leave, not even when we try to lure him with his football. We have to drag him out. Later he lies stiff on his cot in a room with five other boys.

Living Water is a children's home, not an adoption agency, though a very small number of children have been adopted by Americans personally known to the Heinleins. There will be a home for Mash at Living Water for as long as he needs one.

I remember to hand Dr. Heinlein Mash's identification papers — a foolscap form with only his Spanish name, "Tomás." All the other blanks are filled in with "desconocido" — unknown. Will Mash eventually start to talk? I ask.

"Sure. Give him time. Children survive anything, believe me." He points to a five-year-old girl in the next room. A half-smile

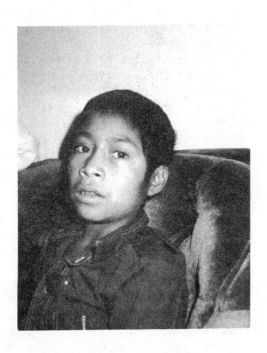

Mash in Nebaj.

flickers on her dreaming face. "She was raped so many times her vagina and anus are now fused into one passage. She'll recover. So will he."

But I can't forget Mash. Three weeks later I make a special trip back from El Salvador to see him.

Mash is sitting alone in a room crowded with kids and dogs and the disarray of cheerful domesticity. The kids crush around us when I hand him a green yoyo I've brought for him. But he does not smile or speak. He is still different, set apart from the other kids.

Can Mash and the other children of war ever become real children — playing, giggling, silly children? I ask Dr. Heinlein.

"What's a child?" he challenges me. "You're judging by your own limited experience.

"Every day, children line up for me, silently, without parents or even a brother or sister to hold their hand. When I examine them I find sores that would make American children scream. But they thank me when I hurt them. They comfort each other.

They wake up smiling when there is nothing to eat but beans. They have no shoes, but they have faith.

"Mash will come out of his trauma, but it could take a year, maybe more. Remember that he saw his parents murdered, and those murderers kept him. When he got used to them, we took him from what had become his security.

"He will eventually begin to trust the world again, that's the magic of being a child. And don't ever underestimate it, because that's the hope of the world. If I didn't believe that, why would I be bouncing up and down mud roads, taking shit from the army?"

Mash's house mother tells me he will soon be going to school, which will make things better for him.

"He seems so much more adult than the other kids. He is very strong, very controlled. He doesn't play."

Has he begun to talk?

"Sort of. He was crying quietly one night and I asked him why he was sad. He wouldn't say, so I asked if it was because of his mum and dad. Were they dead? 'Yes,' he whispered. 'The soldiers shot them.'

"But the next day he climbed up the big tree again — he does that every day, and I can't get him down. I asked him what he was looking out for, and he said, 'They're coming for me. My mum and dad.' "

Licha

Licha and the other widows are shucking beans, sitting back on their heels like dancers, brilliant in their native dress. They look like so many exotic birds — like the Guatemalan national bird, the quetzal, which dies in captivity and is, not surprisingly, almost extinct in Guatemala today.

But the twenty-nine widows of Caserío San Pablo are very much alive. All their men-folk, most of the old folk, and some of their children have been killed in army massacres or have died in the mountains where they fled. Now the women have begun a new life.

I came to the widows' little village in Lower Verapaz with community workers from the Family Centre for Integration, one of the few groups operating in the "pacified zones" where displaced people still wander, outcasts in their own land after years of terror. Nobody knows exactly how many widows there are: nobody is counting and very few are protesting in Guatemala. Figures on how many have been killed or have disappeared since 1954 in Guatemala range from fifty thousand according to Amnesty International, to a hundred thousand according to the Guatemalan Commission on Human Rights.

The youngest widow at Caserío San Pablo is sixteen and the oldest child, ten. I've been warned that the women are very shy and don't speak Spanish, only Kekchí, the local Indian language. I'm told they won't want to talk. So I sit down first with the children at the other end of the open-sided shed, listening to their lessons. Very patiently, the young, male teacher helps forty or fifty children read the verse on the chalkboard and copy it down with stubby fingers:

"*La osa ama a Mama*" — The mother bear loves Mama.

With a heart-wrench I realize that every verse on the board refers to mothers, but never to fathers. "We use what the children know," the teacher explains later. "How would I explain 'father' to children who have no father and don't want to remember what happened to the father they once had? They have mothers, and their mothers are enough."

I watch the mothers shucking beans, their fingers rustling at the dried stalks, their voices soft and throaty while they gaze proudly at the children. When I go over and sit with the busy widows on the floor, Licha speaks to me because she's seen me look at the copy-book of a boy called Lucas, her sister's child.

"My sister died, so Lucas came with me. I only have one child, my baby here." And she swings round so that I can see the sleeping baby in the carrying cloth on her back.

How does she know Spanish?

"I worked in the city, in a house, with a ladino family. But I didn't like it. That was a long time ago, when I was young."

Licha is now eighteen. I ask, as gently as I can, what has happened to her husband.

"He was killed at Río Negro. The soldiers came in helicopters. They lined up all the men. They kept the women in the church and we could not get out. When they opened the door, we found all the men were dead. Some had their heads cut off."

What did the women do then?

"We ran as soon as the soldiers left. We hid in the mountains, but some of the old people could not go very far and others got sick."

I ask how long they were in hiding. Licha guessed a few months. When I check the dates later, I find it was over a year. "We had to eat roots. We boiled leaves. We had to shelter in caves. We went back to our village, but it was all burned. The soldiers hadn't left us even a cooking pot, and I was afraid to stay there in the night. So we kept walking, looking for food. A lot of the children cried all day.

"One woman had a cousin in the village by the river here, so we came down to get help, but the people here didn't speak our language and they didn't like us. We sat by the road. We were very dirty."

José Rossi, co-organizer of the Family Centre that funds the widows' village, confirms that when they appeared late in 1983 the women and their children were starving.

"See if you can find any children older than babies, younger than four. You won't, because they died of hunger."

Now, the widows have beans and corn because they have planted, cultivated, and harvested them themselves, without tools for there is no plough, no scythes. They built their own houses out of cement blocks bought with a $20,000 gift from the Canadian Embassy, arranged by the Family Centre. They built thirty-five houses instead of the twenty-nine they need, so that other women can find a home, too. That was their idea.

"They decided where to put the houses, in this semi-circle. And some of them planted corn right outside the door, which was not how we would have planned it. But it is their village," Rossi comments.

"Two new babies have been born since they came. If they have babies that is their business, we are happy for them. It is our job to protect them as much as we can, not to run their lives."

The widows have delicate faces, slight bodies, small, bare feet. I marvel at the heavy work they've accomplished. "Working the land was very hard," Licha admits. "You see, we had never worked before."

I don't understand what she means, knowing that Indian women are up at dawn making tortillas, fetching water, selling

Licha (far right) in Caserío San Pablo.

produce in the market, and caring for husbands, children, animals.

"That's not real work. That's just women's work," Licha explains.

She says that it is easier now because they have a wheelbarrow. The bean crop has been harvested. The corn is nearly ready. Four pigs and some chickens run through the corn rows. They even have a white, scrawny dog. The Guatemalan flag flies from the pole in front of the community shed where the women work and the children go to school. Some day maybe the women will learn to read and write, as their children have done. But now they have to do men's and women's work. There are clothes to wash in the stream at the edge of the village, food to cook, children to feed.

"We want to be independent," says Licha. "We are going to get fruit trees so we can sell apples. And, if only we could get a sewing machine and some cloth, we could make clothes."

Licha is full of hopes for the future, but the village still looks so pathetic to me, I wonder how she can be so optimistic. Their little houses have no furniture; their beds are made up with rags. Biting flies have given the children conjunctivitis. The civil patrols still terrify those women who venture out onto the road. "What do you talk about, when you are working together?" I ask her, thinking they must have so many bitter memories. She has lost everything that makes life normal for a Guatemalan woman. She has heard the killings and survived the mountains, but has been left with so little security, so fragile a hold on life, so little to hope for.

"We talk about the children, of course."

I ask her what she would do if she could take revenge against the soldiers. Does she hate them?

"If I saw them, I would be very afraid, but what could I do to them? They have guns. When I have to go into the village, I hide if I see a soldier. Or the Civil Guard, too."

I ask José Rossi if the widows' village would ever be integrated into the larger life of the community. What would happen to Licha, a widow at eighteen? Would she always be afraid?

"Hard to say," he admits, "because this is a new situation. These women have never been left on their own like this. They get a lot of strength from each other, but they have always turned to their men for decisions and support.

"So far they are doing very well. They may find new partners, but there will be very few men for them. It's rather like Europe was after the Second World War. If they see the children grow up and learn and get decent food, that will be a new life for them. They will live their own lives through their children."

At dark, the twenty-nine widows gather their children and put out the tiny cooking fires outside their houses. They have no lamps. Do they dream of the men they had loved, or of the men with guns? Do they lie awake? Do they wake up screaming? We will never know. But at least now they sleep in relative safety, with their children beside them.

María

María Chític got mad when they called her a dirty Indian. Then the lady of the house told her she hadn't hung the washing properly on the line. And when María wouldn't drop her floorcloth, get up and rehang the washing immediately, she got fired.

This treatment, of course, is nothing new in Guatemala, where domestic work is women's main source of employment, but a job without many rights. What was new was María's decision to sue her employer for back wages.

I heard about María from the San Carlos University legal clinic, where María applied for help. Through Rolando, her law student counsel, I met María and the neighbour who had helped and encouraged her to demand her rights. Before we met, I had been reading *My Name is Rigoberta Menchú*, the story of an Indian woman leader who had become a domestic servant at the age of twelve.[6] Rigoberta could neither speak Spanish nor read and write. She had no shoes. Her employer kept back her first six months' wages to pay for her shoes, because she did not want her friends to see a dirty, barefoot servant girl in the house. Rigoberta eventually organized a domestic servants' union and went on to join the guerrillas.

María is fighting Rigoberta's battle all over again. As an Indian domestic servant, she was exploited because of her ignorance, and treated like an unloved but useful animal around the house.

But now, when I meet her, María Chític is no longer ignorant and is only half scared. Broad-faced, chunky, and quite composed, she tells me her story in good Spanish and with a shy giggle. She is twenty-two.

"I was born in Santa María Jilotepeque, Chimaltenango. I was the second youngest of eight children and I married when I was seventeen, which is quite late. But after a few years my husband, Pedro, ran off with another woman and I was left with my two daughters, María Dora and Marta Julia, and no way to make a living.

"My mother-in-law came for the children. I didn't know how to stop her taking them, because I could not feed them. So I went to Guatemala City to look for work and I found a job with this military officer and his family. They had four children, so I had a lot to do."

How much did they pay her?

"Ten dollars a week. That's the usual wage. I got up at six in

[6] Elisabeth Burgos-Debray (ed.), *I, Rigoberta Menchú: An Indian Woman in Guatemala* (London: Verso, 1984).

the morning and worked until eleven-thirty at night. They didn't want me to clean up the living room until they had all gone to bed, so I had to wait in the kitchen for them to leave before I could clean up.

"I had to do all the shopping and cooking, all the cleaning, washing, and ironing. They let me have a half day off every Sunday, when I went to see a neighbour, but I couldn't see my little children. I saw them only twice a year, when I had a few days off. I used to save all my money for that.

"The señor wasn't unkind. He did not try to have relations with me, you know what I mean, like many men do with domestic servants. The señora was sometimes good, sometimes bad, depending on the moment. Most of the time she just sat in front of the television.

"The daughters were the worst. They called me a dirty Indian and they laughed at me. They would leave their clothes on the floor and expect me to pick up everything. If I got tired they would say I was lazy. I tried my best and I am a good cook, that is what I like doing. But they were always complaining."

The señora liked to show off María to her friends as "the little Indian girl I took in." She insisted that María wear her native costume, the *huipil*, though sometimes María wanted to keep her *huipiles* clean, for best, and not get them dirty.

"Sometimes she seemed to like me being Indian. Then she would say I was stupid, but I think she wanted me to be ignorant. My friend taught me how to speak Spanish and how to read and write a little bit, but I never told my employers I could read or write because they wouldn't want that. They don't like servants who can read or write. They say city girls are spoiled; country girls are better workers."

María had heard there was a special radio program for the thousands of domestic workers in Guatemala City. It taught them how to plan their fifteen-hour day, how to budget time, how to give themselves rest periods, even how many hours there were in a day. But María never got to listen because she had no radio and was too busy, anyway.

Now, she is suing for two months' back pay and for holiday pay she never received in three years working for that family. It amounts to $110. It was her neighbour's idea to sue, and María Chític is still amazed to find herself talking to a law student and

María Chític.

on the way to court. "I hope the señora won't be there," she says.

But the neighbour encourages her to get her mind off her fears by thinking of the new job she should be getting and her hopes of seeing her children next month. She has been to three interviews for a new job. But she has not told any of the señoras that she can read or write: "That would make them suspicious."

What María Chític would like best of all would be a job where her children could be close to her. It is still far beyond her expectations to think of living with her daughters. But maybe her neighbour would keep her children for her if she could get a job close by and make enough money to pay for her children's board in the city. The neighbour would take the children, if only her mother-in-law would give them up.

María feels she has changed a lot from the day when she first became a domestic servant.

"At first I was so shy I couldn't even talk. I was afraid most of the time. What would I do if I got sick? Would they throw me into the street? Would I ever see my daughters again? Would they hit me if the milk boiled over? Would they get mad if I used too much soap?

"I am not like that now, but I still have to pretend to be stupid or I won't get a job."

Understandably, María has no desire for her daughters to be domestic servants. She'd rather they be teachers. "But how will I find the money to send them to school? First, I have to get them close to me. That is the hardest thing for a mother who is a domestic servant — not being able to live with her own children. They always want you to live in so you will be available all the time, and no family will let you bring the children into the house."

I ask if there is any other work for María Chític that would let her keep her children. I'm told that women working in the textile factories have no unions, no day care, low wages, and no protection against getting fired. Working in the service areas is even less rewarding. I talk to an eighteen-year-old working at McDonalds, where hot dogs are still "hot dogs" in Spanish and hamburgers are *hamburguesas*. She gets three dollars for an eight-hour day.

Prostitution seems to be flourishing, though. The Guatemalan police arrested six hundred women in one night alone while I was in the city. It was both a crackdown on "vice" and a way to check on documentation. No clients were arrested.

A few years ago María Chític would probably have joined the prostitutes, too, after getting fired from her job. The fact that she has decided, instead, to fight for her rights, indicates a new hope for her and her sisters. Later I check with Rolando. María has won her case, is expecting to collect $80, and has got a new job. Her neighbour is trying to arrange for her children to move to Guatemala City so that María can see them once a week.

Lorenzo

Getting to speak to someone like Lorenzo is tough, because the Guatemalan army does not like its soldiers to talk to foreigners. Lorenzo's commanding officer in the Quiché has prohibited any interview. And, after listening to lectures by pompous army public relations men and chatting up commanders who agreed that the soldiers' side of the civil war should be told, but not by one of their men, I am about to give up.

It is quite by accident that I find myself, for more than an hour, sharing a waiting-room bench with Lorenzo Mejía. Lorenzo is a sergeant with a kamikaze platoon badge on his beret. Aged eighteen, he is still more boy than soldier, a friendly boy, yet he commands twenty men. He wears camouflage fatigues and carries himself proudly, a handsome young man with curiously light green eyes and black hair. We begin by talking about his childhood. He was born in Cobán, in Alta Verapaz, but his parents sent him away to live with his uncle in the Petén when he was a kid. "I don't know why. I don't remember them very much, only that my dad yelled at me a lot. There were a lot of children. Maybe they didn't have room for us all."

Lorenzo liked the Petén, with its wild animals — "what we call the tiger [the jaguar] and monkeys and big fish in the river." The jungle was all around the little town he lived in. "If you went a few steps outside, you would be lost in a big, green world. You couldn't see the sun because the trees were so big they covered the sky. I ran around all day.

"Sometimes my uncle would take me hunting. He had a gun, but he wouldn't let me use it. It was only a hunting gun. I used to dream of having my own gun."

Getting a gun wasn't the only reason Lorenzo was happy to join the army at age seventeen. He wanted to be with other boys. Anyway, seventeen is the age to start military service. Lots of boys become soldiers earlier, through the common practice of forced recruitment. Army trucks descend on Indian villages at fiesta time or on market day to capture recruits. Without proper identification, it is impossible for a boy to prove he is under seventeen. In Guatemala City I have seen army trucks packed with boys and guarded by soldiers with machine-guns. The boys are barely five feet tall, and they are silent. But how do you tell how old someone is in a land of malnutrition, where even the elite guard outside the presidential palace, weighed down with guns, two-way radios, and ropes for tying up prisoners, look like children?

Lorenzo is five feet six inches tall and well-built. He likes the physical activity of the army and the challenge of getting the men in his platoon fit enough for jungle warfare. In two weeks, he says, he trained them to be able to march twenty-five kilometres with full pack, and then fight.

"They were soft when they came. No discipline. I was lucky because I was used to physical activity in the Petén."

Lorenzo thinks he might stay on in the army. Or else he might get work with the police, or as a security guard, or with one of the many semi-official rural armies that make Guatemala a militarized state. "There are lots of jobs for somebody who can use a gun," he says.

Lorenzo has an Israeli-made Uzi machine-gun, but not with him now, because he is not on duty. I ask him if he has ever killed anyone. He hesitates.

"I don't know. I've used my gun, yes. But I don't know if I have killed anyone. It isn't like the movies. You keep shooting and some terrorists fall down, but I don't know if it was me that shot them."

How would he feel if he knew he had killed? Would it bother him?

"Not killing terrorists. We've got to eliminate them. They've killed thousands of peasants. They are Communists and they want to take over the country. They don't believe in God."

Does Lorenzo believe? Does he go to church? Yes, he believes in God, but he doesn't go to church and he isn't sure if it is a sin to kill.

"That can't be true for the army, because the army has to protect the country. There are Cubans and Communists everywhere. I know that. Two hundred Cubans were killed by the army only a few months ago, near San Marcos."

I tell him that is impossible. He doesn't believe me. Are there Russians in Guatemala, too? I ask.

"I don't think so, but they pay the subversives. They are traitors. We are the patriots."

I tell him that the world press has published verified accounts of Guatemalan massacres: stories of children bayoneted, peasants burned alive, and villages wiped out. There is evidence, I say, of army commanders competing in the number of peasants their men killed in a week.

"Communist lies," Lorenzo insists. "You must be mad to believe that." But the conversation is making him noticeably uncomfortable, so I switch subject and ask him what he does in his free time.

"We have volley-ball and football, and movies in the bar-

Lorenzo Mejía in
Nebaj.

racks. We don't need to go into the town."

What about girls?

"We keep ourselves clean," he replies, and when I fail to understand the connection, he flushes, embarrassed. "The girls here are prostitutes."

Lorenzo doesn't have much to spend, anyway. His army pay is $20 a month. Another $20 goes to his uncle, who is listed as his immediate family. Twice a year he gets leave, but it is too difficult for him to get to where his uncle lives so he stays in the barracks. He is not keen on looking for his mother or father because they haven't bothered in years to keep in touch with him.

"I have all I want in the army. It has given me a real pride in myself. We have classes in arithmetic, and Spanish grammar, and public health, and traditional values, things like that."

Later on I inspect some of the school books used by the army for new recruits. They aren't nearly as heavy on politics or patriotism as I expected; how to clean your teeth, and the etiquette of giving up a seat on the bus to women and the elderly take up more space than any anti-communist propaganda or lectures on the national flag.

"We don't get lectures on patriotism. We learn by example," says Lorenzo. I tell him that I have read stories of Guatemalan army recruits being brainwashed so that they would readily kill their own fellow-countrymen. He looks at me as if I am mad, and shuffles his feet. I shift to something less threatening — army food. Is it good?

Lorenzo has no complaints about the food. I tell him I have just come back from a clinic where children are dying from malnutrition; children who were supposed to be properly fed in the army-controlled camps they call "poles of development" (the old term of "strategic hamlets" smacks too much of the days of Viet Nam).

"That's the terrorists' fault," Lorenzo promptly claims. "There would be no displaced people if the terrorists hadn't come. Now the army has to build roads and villages and bring in food and medicine. Everybody blames the army, but we can't do everything. We don't even get help from the Yankees, and that is not fair."

Again I try to bridge the gap I've created by my clumsy questioning. I tell him I have four sons.

"Can they shoot? Are they in the army?" Disappointed by my response, he loses interest, and tells me he has to go. Standing up, he becomes instantly sure of himself, once again a sergeant. His "*adiós*" is a dismissal. He even smiles.

Nanci

Nanci de la Férrea, aged thirteen, is walking beside me on the first march that families of the disappeared in Guatemala have dared to make. Her dad, Hugo, a teacher, disappeared on his way to work five months previously, and there has been no trace of him since then.

Nanci walks with her mother, but she is still scared. When a TV camera-crew drives alongside us, she ducks under the placard she is carrying. The sign reads, "Where are you, Papa? We need you." A too-large baseball cap already obscures her eyes, but she is still afraid of somebody recognizing her. "I don't want my friends to see me," she whispers. "They don't know my dad is missing. I just told them he was away, working."

Her mother is just as scared. So are the thousand other marchers who have set out one Saturday morning at dawn from the little town of San Lucas Sacatepequez, twenty-six kilometres down the highway from Guatemala City. They formed their group only six months ago and the name they have chosen indicates the climate of fear in Guatemala: "The Group of Mutual Support for the Appearance, with Life, of our Children, Husbands, Fathers, and Brothers." There is no mention even of disappearances. There is no protest; no finger is pointed at the authorities responsible for the many killings and disappearances. No one knows how many have disappeared or have been killed. Even Amnesty International, the United Nations, and the International Red Cross have no reliable figures. Maybe fifty thousand have been killed and kidnapped, maybe a hundred thousand.

In Chile, the families of the disappeared began protesting in 1975, two years after the military coup that overthrew President Salvador Allende's socialist government. In Argentina, the Mad Mothers of the Plaza de Mayo began their white-kerchiefed protests in 1976. This was the first action of a protest that became a movement in Argentina; a movement that finally ousted the military from power in 1983. Even in El Salvador, the mothers of the disappeared hold regular protests, sitting on the Cathedral steps, appealing to the Supreme Court, even to the U.S. ambassador, to find out what happened to their kidnapped families.

But in Guatemala, until now, there has been no protest. Terror rules the streets. Each morning the newspapers report the body count of the day before — the bodies of professors and prostitutes, taxi-drivers, teachers, and once, even a U.S. Peace Corps member. The agony is indiscriminate. Police arrest other policemen. Bodyguards shoot it out with rivals. If you walk home after an eight o'clock movie, you are asking for a bullet in the back. In the countryside, whole villages are wiped out. There, nobody reports the killings.

President Oscar Mejía Víctores insists, not surprisingly, that there are no killings, no political prisoners, no disappeared.

"These people like to travel," he said when questioned on the fate of the disappeared in July 1984. "They will probably come back to Guatemala with different names. We have no responsibility."

But the relatives of the disappeared have begun files on 250 people whose arrest has been witnessed by neighbours who saw them dragged from their homes by civilians and stuffed into cars later traced to the police. Sometimes the uniformed police have arrested the victim. Sometimes relatives saw a man in jail. But the authorities never admitted that such prisoners are being held, and the prisoners never come home. The Guatemalan government insists it has no political prisoners.

Members of the Mutual Support group still have faith that their loved ones are in some jail. In September 1984 they had gathered enough courage to hold a press conference. Now, with witnesses from the International Peace Brigade, a pacifist group, they are on their first march. It is a march for peace, as this is the only way to stage such a demonstration.

Even so, Archbishop Próspero Penados del Barrio has already voiced his concern that the families might try to take over his cathedral, cause a disturbance, and turn the peace march into a protest against a government he does not care to confront.

"The Archbishop is no better than the army," mutters Nanci when we discuss the newspaper report of what the Archbishop said. Her mother glares at her, but Nanci goes on. "Well, he could speak up if he wanted to, couldn't he? And he says nothing."

"Don't you believe the church is on the side of people like you?" I ask.

"God is. The church isn't. Not here. They are too scared."

It is true, the church in Guatemala is scared. They have good reason to be afraid. Twelve priests and about ten thousand catechists and other lay workers have been killed since the church began, in the 1960s, to protest atrocities. In 1980, the Bishop of El Quiché had to close down every church in his region because of death threats to his priests. Even Pope John Paul II cut no ice with the Guatemalan regime when, a week before his visit to Guatemala in 1983, he formally interceded for the lives of six young people about to be executed. They were shot anyway a couple of days before he arrived.

And yet a dozen Franciscan friars march alongside us in san-

Nanci de la Férrea.

dals and brown habits, and I later discover two other priests marching. None want their names published.

Most of the marchers are women, Indian women. Many of them are barefoot, some of them with babies wrapped in carrying clothes on their backs, and all in the brightly woven *huipiles* of their villages. They clutch the hands of their older children.

"I feel sorry for the kids. My little brother is only five, and he still can't understand why his dad doesn't come home like other fathers do," says Nanci.

Her mother is having a hard time, financially. Although she works as a secretary in a school, she has no savings, no pension, no government assistance. She can not, and will not, claim that her husband is dead. She is in limbo, not knowing the truth, never wanting to give up hope.

"It isn't fair," Nanci rages. "It just isn't fair." I decide to ask her if she is angry at the men who took her father away one morning on his way to school. Does she want revenge? Nanci is puzzled.

"Revenge against whom? I don't know who they were or where to find them. But I am angry. Sometimes I feel angry at everybody. But, even so, I don't want to hurt anybody."

But if you were in the same room with the man who took your father away and you had a gun, wouldn't you shoot him? "No. I'd be too afraid. I wouldn't know what to do. All I want is to have him back again," she responds.

Nanci is a good student who wants to be a teacher — "like my dad." She likes Michael Jackson records, doesn't like having to look after her kid brother, hates washing up, but enjoys sewing and helping her mother. She says she doesn't know anything about politics, and thinks that kids shouldn't get mixed up in things that could be dangerous.

When the march, hot and weary, reaches the outskirts of Guatemala City, Nanci becomes obviously more nervous. Her eyes flicker from street corner to street corner where army trucks might be waiting.

Some of the marchers become more vocal, especially the contingent of workers who have been locked out of the Coca Cola plant. They shout out: "*El Pueblo Unido Jamás Será Vencido*" [The People United Will Never Be Defeated]. This was the rallying-cry of Salvador Allende, killed in Chile in 1973.

Outside the Presidential Palace the march halts. Three women go in to present a petition to the President, but find nobody at work except for the ubiquitous guards with their Galil sub-machine-guns. For a few moments everyone is nonplussed. The marchers line up, not knowing what to do. The three women finally give the petition to the guards. Somebody hands around white carnations. The marchers throw them as hard as they can at the staring guards, and the flowers flutter forlornly onto the palace steps. Some of the women are crying. Finally, the march moves off in the direction of the cathedral.

In the cathedral, the marchers overflow the seats and many kneel humbly on the stone floor. The Archbishop prays for peace to descend from the heavens upon stricken Guatemala. He never once mentions the disappeared, their desperate families, or who is responsible for their misery. Two Indian men in front of me, their hunched, narrow shoulders in threadbare jackets, bow their heads patiently. They still believe in a God of goodness. Then we all file out, tired, let down, but relieved there has been no repression. That alone means the march is a success. Some people are already talking about future protests, and asking how they can get more church support.[7]

I ask Nanci what she will tell her friends at school about the march. "But they won't know I was here," she answers. "I just hope they won't ever know."

Carlos

Carlos, aged fifteen, is happy in school and doesn't want to go home. Home means the town of Chiquimula, where an educated Indian would come under immediate suspicion. The military would want to know why he had been to school in Guatemala City for three years, and why he has come home.

"It won't be easy, trying to make a living," he tells me. "When I go home now, twice a year, they always ask questions about me."

Carlos goes to school at the Indigenous Institute, twelve kilometres from Guatemala City. Run by the Christian Brothers, the Institute accommodates and teaches 185 Indian boys. Most of them are sent to the Institute when they are twelve. Local priests watch out for promising boys who can speak some Spanish, are leaders of their group, and are good students. The chosen ones stay at the school six years, getting a good education and learning the fundamentals of many skills, such as carpentry, tailoring, agriculture, weaving, baking, and metal work. They specialize in one skill so that they can later earn a living at home, but the most important thing the Brothers teach them is pride in being Indian. Brother Oscar Ismitia of the Institute explains:

"These boys here are the descendants of the Mayans who

---

[7] In March 1985, Héctor Gómez, a founder of the Mutual Support Group, was found murdered, his tongue ripped out. In April 1985, another founder, María Rosario Godoy, and her infant disappeared. Later they were found dead. The baby's fingernails had been pulled out. General Mejía Víctores later declared: "To take steps towards the reappearance alive of the disappeared is a subversive act, and measures will be adopted to deal with it."

invented the calendar. The Mayans knew astronomy, wrote books, and built cities like Tikal: cities that tourists now pay thousands of dollars to go and see. But, when they come here, all they know about being Indian is that it is a bad thing to be. Indians may be the majority in this country, but ever since the Spanish conquest they have been derided, exploited, and treated like animals. It is no wonder they have an inferiority complex.

"Today, discrimination against Indians in Guatemala has reached the level of genocide. The authorities pick off anybody who shows signs of being a leader. This makes it essential not only to create new leaders but also to teach them survival skills.

"All these boys are trained to be rural educators, so they can help their community rise up out of its misery. This means being able to communicate ideas and to organize people, but, above all, it means being able to survive. That is why they all learn a useful skill. They know they won't get jobs as teachers. There aren't many schools open in Indian villages, and, in the few that do exist, the teacher has to do as he is told or he won't last very long.

"Here the boys learn pride. They learn how to function in a difficult reality. What good would it do to train brave young men to go and get killed?

"This is a Christian school. We do not believe in violence. We believe in brotherly love — and good sense."

With my introduction to the Institute over, Brother Ismitia leads me outside where we meet Carlos, a poised young man in a uniform of blue jeans, white T-shirt, and sneakers. In fact, the whole Institute looks more like a private boys' college than a charity school. Set back from the highway, it has basketball courts and a football field alongside the pasture where black and white cows graze. The classrooms are bright and modern, and the dormitories are new. Even the pig-sties are well-kept, with hardly a straw on the concrete runways.

Carlos shows me the pigs, but without affection. He doesn't like pigs, even the bright ones, but he recognizes it is useful for all the boys to take a turn in agricultural work in their first two years. He does like working in the corn fields because the Institute is experimenting with various hybrid corn, and is not just growing food for the kitchens.

But he enjoys woodwork best. He has made beds with round legs, he informs me. Maybe he will specialize in carpentry.

Carlos really wants to become a teacher, but he knows he will never get a teaching job. Still he hopes that maybe, one day, things will change. He likes his lessons. Best of all, he likes projects concerning his own native origins:

"We are asked to translate legends of our people into Spanish. Well, I hardly knew any legends. I had to ask around in the village; only two old men knew any stories. They are about tricks and jokes played on the rich men. I translated some of them into Spanish, and we all had a lot of fun."

His best subject, though, is music. He takes me into the practice room, where some forty boys are playing guitar and charango. Four lucky boys play the marimba — the waist-high wooden instrument that is Guatemala's own. It looks a little like a dulcimer. At one time, every village had a marimba for entertainment. Now it is used mainly to entertain tourists.

I tell Carlos about the luxury hotel in Chichicastenango, where the waiters wear native dress with scarlet embroidered pants and elaborate head-dresses, and where the marimba plays all day.

"I don't like to see things like that," he says. "They use Indians when they want to look good, like in the beauty contests. But they are hypocrites. They use us and then they kill us."

Whom is he talking about? Who are "they"? Carlos looks uncomfortable and falls silent.

Is there anything he doesn't like about the school? I ask, switching subjects.

The food is too much the same, though it is plentiful. Carlos hesitates, and then he adds, "I wish we had some girls."

Later, I bring this issue up with Brother Ismitia. He obviously recognizes the dangers of bringing up boys for six years in a monastic atmosphere, then letting them loose, but he sees no option. "We're not educating them for the priesthood. We would like to have girls too, but we are working within the Guatemalan tradition and the church has always educated boys and girls separately."

One good thing is that his students have, so far, been able to escape the army draft. The authorities have left the Institute alone. This means not only no harassment but also no government economic or moral support. The Institute depends entirely upon the Catholic church, since the boys cannot afford any

school fees. But they feel lucky to avoid government notice.
"Being a closed society allows us to take a boy out of a harmful environment. Back home, there isn't just ignorance, there is alcoholism, there are drugs, there is repression and despair. It is only by putting the boys into a different setting that they are able to develop their potential, and the strength to go back home and face reality."

Carlos, like many of the boys, doesn't have strong family ties. His father is "somewhere in Mexico," one of thousands of Guatemalan refugees. His mother is dead. When he goes home he stays with a sister. He never writes to her because she can't read.

"I don't think much about my old friends. I'm different from the boy who came here three years ago. Why, then I was so scared I thought the first bus I saw at night was attacking me! Now I'm part of a basketball team that is the best in the district. Everybody expects a lot from me. That's frightening, but it is exciting, too.

"Whatever happens, I won't let the Brothers down. They have faith in me."

María Elena

Imagine this is your first job as a social worker. You are in charge of 171 widows who are being threatened by armed men, and it is up to you to protest to the army commander. You are only twenty years old. That is what María Elena Chávez Ixcaguic faces in Cerro Alto, just outside the tourist town of Chichicastenango.

Barely five feet tall, María is the director of the local community centre organized by REDH Integral (Reconstruction and Integrated Human Development), one of a very few independent organizations encouraging self-help and education for change.

She began her work two years ago, straight after a year's course in social work, and is now the person everybody comes to with their problems.

The milk from the UN food fund hasn't come in. Twelve more kids, abandoned or orphaned, have wandered into the house. The dispensary is out of cough medicine. No seed has come for the vegetable garden project. A boy is missing. The accounts haven't been done. No budget was prepared for the building project, so no funds are available. And the dog has bitten a fruit-vendor.

"I'm not very good at this, am I?" she asks, pushing back a lock of long black hair behind one of her two barrettes. "I'm sure somebody else could do this much better than I can."

But Adolfo Acosta, director of REDH, has perfect confidence in María's abilities. The problem is, there is so much to do there is never time to plan ahead, that's all.

María Elena has to walk six miles a day, from village to village. Maybe a motorbike would be the answer, Adolfo suggests. Can she ride one?

"Sure, why not? It would be better than using the truck, because we need that for delivering food, and it is a waste when there is just me."

María Elena has no fear of getting lost, no apprehensions of getting stranded on the barely passable road or being washed away in flash floods. "All the local people know me. I'm one of them, a Quiché. I speak their language and I wear their dress, my own native dress. In school, my friends asked why I still kept my *traje* when they wore 'white' clothes. But I wouldn't change because I'm proud to be Indian. That's why they trust me here."

Because her father and mother died when she was fourteen, María Elena also knows the heartache of being deserted. Her grandmother took her and her five brothers and sisters into her home, but that wasn't the same as having parents, and María Elena still misses her parents. She is a soft touch for abandoned kids.

Twenty-four of them live in an office, with living quarters for three. From babies to fourteen-year-olds, they swarm in the little courtyard and tangle in the flapping lines of washing. María Elena picks up Pocha, aged two.

"She couldn't speak when she was brought in. Couldn't walk, either. She was like a doll. Another little girl carried her on her back. Nobody knows who her parents are or where she's from. Now she is running around. Her real name, the children say, is Sebastiana, but they call her Pocha and so that's what we call her."

The kids sleep four to a bed, leaving no space for María Elena so she sleeps on the floor. The office space is crammed with food for distribution (some from the U.S. AID and some from the UN, including milk and wheat flour from Canada). Community Centre activities include a milk program, health and nutrition classes for mothers, a literacy class, sewing and embroidery classes, a typing class (attended only by teenage boys and taught by a fourteen-year-old boy), a demonstration agricultural plot to improve corn and vegetable production, a dispensary and medical clinic, and, now, a new program for displaced widows. This last is María Elena's particular concern.

Later, we drive out to Xepocol, where five young widows are cooking a midday meal for all the widows and children in the immediate area. María Elena provides most of the food, although the women have started to grow vegetables behind the thatched-roof hut. But few of the widows have come for the meal. What is wrong? The women all start talking at once. María Elena sits down and listens.

It is the civil patrols, again, they say. These are local men, organized and given guns by the army, who are forced to patrol one day a week for twenty-four hours, without pay. This is Guatemala's method of enforcing order and also of winning the "loyalty" of peasants who were strong supporters of the guerrillas two or three years ago. Now, those who have not been killed have to help the army against their own people, or they could be killed themselves. This kind of execution has actually happened at least once, when members of a civil patrol refused to kill local peasants and were themselves executed by the army.

Every village in the north of Guatemala is guarded by civil patrols; nobody can enter or leave without their permission. Access to guns and power has corrupted some of them, who have used their arms to terrorize local people. This is happening at Xepocol.

"They told the widows that they should not be allowed free meals because the women were widows of subversives. That meant they were subversives themselves. And their children should not be allowed in the schools. So the women were really scared. And now they won't come down from their homes, and the children are going hungry," said María Elena. "What do I do?" she asks Adolfo Acosta.

"You'll have to go and see the military commander and complain," he replies. María Elena makes a face. But she will go next morning.

47

María Elena.

"Sometimes the civil guards punish women by putting them in holes in the ground and keeping them there all night. They do that if the women refuse to go to bed with them. Another day they thought the widows here were laughing at them, so they beat them. You can't even laugh without permission, here. Nobody likes the civil guard, but the worst of it is that they are our own people, the old men and the boys who grew up here. They don't want to make war on the peasants, but they are under the control of the army."

I heard stories about abuses by the civil patrols all through the Quiché. On the way to Nebaj our bus was stopped at seven check-points manned by patrolmen. They checked identity cards, not once smiling even though most of the passengers were local people. There was no conversation.

María Elena is clearly nervous about having to meet the army commander to complain about the civil patrols at Xepocol. Surely he wouldn't want them bullying the women? she wonders aloud. Or is it the army commander himself who has ordered this type of threat to keep the local people in check? Whatever his responsibility in this, he is the man she will have to see.

"It won't always be like this," she says quietly, and begins to talk about her organization's plans for the widows and children. They are going to build homes for those widows who are willing to take in two or three orphans, besides their own children. These will be real families, where the kids can grow up like normal kids, and the mothers will have the work they know best — mothering. They have already cleared the ground. There will be an orchard, and rabbits, too.

"I see the children come into town, in rags, and I want to cry. But I don't have time."

Is it fair for somebody so young to have such a load of responsibility? I ask.

"Nothing is fair in Guatemala," she replies. Yes, she wants to have fun, go to movies, go out with a boyfriend, get married. But, she says, she is already a spinster, *soltera*, at twenty. "Anyway, there aren't any young men, not for us. They are all dead." So she doesn't think about marriage, at least not very much.

"I have my children, here. I have too many of them, that's the trouble. What I wish is that I had time to love them all."

Angela's Orphans

They call them "Angela's orphans," which is incorrect, because most of them aren't orphans at all, and they certainly don't belong to Angela de Galdámez, director of the Casa Guatemala in Guatemala City.

Some hundred children, from five days to fifteen years old, swarm through the three big houses and spill out into the courtyards of the Casa Guatemala. The Casa is located in an upper-class area of the city, close to the U.S. Embassy. Most of the children have come here from hospitals. The rest are from juvenile courts or have been sent by social workers. Most of them have families and somewhere to return home. But, when they first arrive here, they look like African famine victims. So dehydrated that their skin hangs in folds over their sharp ribs and stick legs, they lie, dwarfed by their cribs. Two-year-olds weigh five pounds. A seven-year-old weighs only fifteen pounds and is quietly dying.

"Do you want statistics?" asks Angela, a Honduran woman with four children of her own. She visited Casa Guatemala four years ago and could not get the children out of her mind. She stayed to work with them.

"Eight children out of a hundred die of starvation before they reach the age of one. And out of every hundred kids, only thirty-five make it to age eighteen. That's Guatemala."

This happens because in Guatemala 2 per cent of the population owns 70 per cent of the land, and most peasants own nothing. According to the Nutritional Institute for Central America and Panama (INCAP), Guatemalans need $10.40 a day to feed an average family. The minimum wage is now $3.20 a day, and unemployment runs at 52 per cent.

Angela is anything but political. She comes from the upper class and her concerns are purely humanitarian, but even so her efforts to help children have got her into trouble with Guatemala's military government.

"I allowed a local newspaper photographer to take pictures of some babies suffering from malnutrition, and they published them. Next thing I heard was a letter from the President of the Supreme Court, warning me never again to let a photographer into Casa Guatemala.

"He said that the photographs showed a 'negative image.' What is more, they could be detrimental to the self-image of the children concerned. If I wanted to keep Casa Guatemala open, I should make sure that only photographs showing a positive image were published."

I hesitate before taking photographs of a little boy suffering from the skin lesions of kwashiorkor, a condition rarely met outside African famine areas. But Angela encourages me.

"Go ahead. Take it. I've had that letter pinned up on the wall to remind me how the government feels, but I'm not paying any attention to it. I almost feel proud." What upsets her much more than government displeasure is the lack of concern for children among those Guatemalans who could spare the money but don't want to know about hunger and sickness. "When I show pictures to my friends, they don't believe me. Or they say, 'Take that away. It's ugly.' They go to fashion shows and health clubs. They don't seem to feel any responsibility at all for these children."

Indeed, after trying to raise money locally, Angela got only a cheque for $25 from Texaco and for $100 from the largest department store in the country. That was all. Almost all the support for Casa Guatemala comes from outside the country, either in donations or from sponsors who pay $20 a month per child.

"In fact, the authorities told me the only reason they let me run this home was because I am Honduran and could bring in money from outside the country. They didn't even want Guatemalans to contribute, much less offer government money for the work the government should be doing anyway."

Every year, Casa Guatemala needs 1,280 pairs of pyjamas, 600 sweaters, 23,000 cloth diapers, as well as towels, socks, diaper pins, and baby bottles. Last year, 317 children in the home and another 1,328 out-patient kids got medical attention. Twenty-one babies died because they were too far gone to be helped by oral rehydration or intravenous feeding.

In Honduras and Nicaragua I found oral rehydration programs that taught women how to make their own "*Super Limonada*" to cure dehydration from diarrhoea. "Just as salty as a tear, as sweet as a kiss," said the instructions for adding salt and sugar to boiled water. If there was any program at all like this in Guatemala, I failed to find it, though in neighbouring Honduras this cheap remedy was saving thousands of lives.

Guatemalan solutions to human problems are not so very humane. After reading news about the number of abandoned children, politicians campaigning for Guatemala's first elections in thirty years got their names in the papers by donating a few hundred dollars to a children's fund set up by local businessmen. But a major editorial suggested an easier solution to the problem of unwanted kids: wholesale adoptions offered to the United States, where "couples are ready to pay very handsomely for children."

Boy in the Nebaj
market.

I am reminded of the Guatemala City concept of rabies control for dogs. After a newspaper warning that reached only those
few who could afford a newspaper, the police offered strych-
nine pellets to all dogs found on the street. There were dead
dogs in every gutter: problem solved.

Some Guatemalans seem to me to be so ugly, so uncaring.
In the cold rain of Sixth Avenue, downtown, outside a porno
movie house showing *The Damp Dreams of Doris*, I came across a
seven-year-old boy without shoes sheltering his little sister under
a piece of plastic. I gave them the equivalent of twenty-five cents
and hurried to a Chinese dinner. When I walked back, nearly
two hours later, they were still there, waiting, they said, for an
older brother to come and take them home. Only two other
people had given them money and neither of them had asked

what was wrong, why they were there.

Guatemala's tragedy seems to me not only that of cruelty, but of indifference. Otto René Castillo, a Guatemalan poet who was burned alive by the army in 1967 after his guerrilla troop was captured, put it this way, in his poem *Report of an Injustice*:

> Worst of all is the habit.
> Man loses his humanity
> and is no longer concerned
> with the huge pain of another,
> and he eats,
> he laughs,
> he forgets everything.
> I don't want these things
> for my country.
> I don't want these things
> for anyone.[8]

---

[8] Otto René Castillo, "Report of an Injustice," from *Latin American Revolutionary Poetry*, translated by M. Randall and R. Marquez (New York: Monthly Review Press, 1974).

■
Part Two

EL SALVADOR

SAN SALVADOR could be any southern U.S. city, so long as you drive fast from the airport to the Camino Real or Sheraton Hotel downtown. You can drive fast because a toll fee keeps away any horse-drawn traffic, and the highway has been straightened out to avoid the spot where four U.S. churchwomen were murdered by Salvadorean troops in December 1980. Houses on the edge of town sparkle white in a foam of flowering shrubs, so you barely see the barbed wire on top of the walls, or the roving Doberman guard-dogs.

But, inevitably, cracks appear in this comfortable image. Out the car window you see shacks knocked together from boards and plastic, barefoot children, an old man leading a lame horse that drags a water cart, a car with three coffins perched on the roof. Despite a certain downtown glitter San Salvador remains, as poet Manlio Argueta called it, "the butcher's shop of the world."[9]

But, unlike Guatemala City, San Salvador does not smell of fear, it does not hold its breath. It smells, frankly, of sweat, and is the noisiest place I've ever visited. From the window of my cheap hotel, next door to the wrestling arena, I look down on a sea of Salvadoreans, all shouting, selling, buying, arguing, running, and pushing. Two million people are packed into the capi-

[9] Manlio Argueta from his poem "El Poeta Como Pequeño Dios," published in translation in *This Magazine* (Toronto), February/March 1982.

tal city, and five million into a country no larger than Prince Edward Island or the state of Maine. Salvadoreans never seem to sit down or keep quiet. On bus trips, three radios inevitably blare music from three different stations. Passengers shout incessantly to each other above the din.

Downtown, people live fourteen to an apartment. Everybody seems to be scrambling for a living: cadging, bargaining, selling, and quarrelling in the way of overcrowded families. Street noises keep me awake past midnight and wake me again at five in the morning.

The Salvadorean poet Roque Dalton wrote this "love poem" to his fellow-countrymen:

> The spongers, the beggars, the pot-heads
> the stupid sons of whores,
> those who were barely able to get back
> those who had a little more luck
> the forever undocumented
> those who do anything, sell anything, eat anything,
> the first ones to pull a knife,
> the wretched, the most wretched of the wretched,
> my compatriots, my brothers.[10]

Other Central Americans call the Salvadoreans *guanacos* — a beast of burden like a small donkey, and just as intractable. Fame for hard work has indeed become El Salvador's heritage. Its misty Indian past, when it was known as "the land of precious things," died with the 1932 massacre of thirty thousand peasants, most of them Indians. A February 4, 1932 headline in *La Prensa* read:

"The Indian has been, is and will be the enemy of the ladino."

Salvadorean peasants, ever resourceful, quickly dropped their Indian languages, forgot their customs, and dressed "white" or ladino. But that wasn't enough to stop the repression.

The main problem in El Salvador has always been land; there is too little for too many people. Two per cent of the population owns fifty-eight per cent of the land: these are the famous fourteen families that run Salvadorean export agriculture. Eco-

[10] Roque Dalton, "Love Poem," from *Poems*, translated by Richard Schaaf (Willimantic, Conn.: Curbstone Press, 1984).

nomic and social injustice remains the root cause of the Salvadorean revolution. Coffee, cotton, and sugar have made the landowners rich, and have forced peasants off their land and into work gangs on the plantations for the few months of harvest when there is work. A growing industrialization, encouraged by the U.S. Alliance for Progress in the 1960s, has benefited foreign firms but not the local people. They cannot afford to buy the products they make — computer chips, brassieres, Coca-Cola, and cars.

During the 1960s, unions became more militant, in the countryside as well as the city. A war with Honduras in 1969 erupted because of land hunger and unemployment, as Salvadoreans working in Honduras threatened the landowners in that country. In fact, what the press called the "Soccer War," which erupted after violence at a Honduras-El Salvador soccer game, was more truly a landlords' war, a consequence of the land concentration policies of the major landowners on both sides of the border.

Death squads were the right wing's answer to the growing discontent. An electoral fraud in 1972 that reversed the victory of the Christian Democrat José Napoleón Duarte inflamed the resistance as people lost all confidence in the possibility of electoral change. Catholic church leaders began to protest and were murdered or accused of Communist subversion. When it was no longer safe to register an opposition political party, or even to join a neighbourhood association or a more radical union, the people began to join guerrilla groups and take up armed struggle as the only means left for any change.

In 1979, General Carlos Romero was overthrown by younger officers, who formed a junta promising reform. But the oligarchy and the army were not about to give in. Most of the junta resigned within a year, and aligned themselves with the guerrilla groups. During 1980, these many small guerrilla groups united as the Farabundo Martí National Liberation Front (FMLN), with the Democratic Revolution Front (FDR) as its political and diplomatic counterpart. The new organization attracted other groups, professional organizations, student bodies, and unions, making the FMLN and the FDR a broadly-based and popular revolutionary movement.

Since then, El Salvador's war against its own people has cost fifty thousand lives. According to President Duarte, the United

States spends more than a million dollars a day to finance one side in the war. The Reagan administration sees it as a fight against Communism supposedly being spread — along with guns — from Nicaragua. The country is now divided: one-third, the east, is guerrilla territory, one-third is under dispute, and one-third, the rich cotton and sugar lands of the west, is firmly in army hands. There is stalemate in the conflict, stagnation in the economy, impotence in government, and continuing chaos in which the death squads flourish and innocent civilians die.

Now, on my third trip to El Salvador since 1981, I notice how tired everybody is of the war. That is why the first dialogue between the government and the FDR/FMLN guerrillas in 1984 aroused such unrealistic euphoria, as if waving white flags could solve centuries of injustice.

A few figures show why there is a revolution in El Salvador. Only twenty per cent of the people have full employment. Another fifty per cent work only a few months in a year. Infant mortality has risen since 1979 to seventy-five per thousand (in Canada it is nine). Per capita income is $700 a year, six per cent of the Canadian figure. Seventy per cent of the children suffer from malnutrition. Food prices have risen by 97.7 per cent since 1979, and wages have been frozen since 1980. Public spending on education and public health is down by twenty per cent and defence spending is up by nearly two hundred per cent.

Elections have not helped. It is obvious to me that no Salvadoreans, apart from politicians, have any confidence in their government's ability to effect real change, given the intransigence of the right-wing rich, and the foreign policy of the United States.

"Voting does not make democracy," declared the Salvadorean Roman Catholic Bishops' Conference just after the March 1984 elections. For fifty years, elections in El Salvador have failed to achieve any social or economic improvement in the lives of most people. While it is difficult to assess support for the FDR/FMLN, since this is not something you can enquire about openly, it is quite clear that votes cast for the ruling Christian Democrats or their right-wing opposition, the ARENA party, do not necessarily imply any confidence in their policies.

"We get the day off. We have to vote. It is an old, old game. We play it because it is safest to do so, but we know it is a game," a bank teller told me.

But there is another way, a more personal way, to measure the loyalties of the ordinary people, and their support of the guerrillas. San Salvador's crowded population makes it impossible to hide out unless you are a welcome guest. Everybody knows you. I start wandering around the city and seeing the hidden life: the tortilla seller who carries pamphlets in her basket, the man who collects boots for the FMLN *muchachos*, the nuns who look after refugees in their basement and keep an eye on the prostitutes in the house behind them. In turn the prostitutes pump their military clients for information. This is one El Salvador: scared, poverty-stricken, not always political, but fiercely loyal to the neighbourhood, and as fiercely opposed to the authorities who control their lives and kill their young men, the *muchachos*.

The next day I meet a journalist at the Camino Real Hotel. There is a fashion show going on around the pool. Tickets cost $50. Some politicians are there with their wives. Bodyguards in reflecting sunglasses lounge at the bar, guns bulging from their belts. This is the other El Salvador.

I finger the folder in my purse, where I've put photographs of death-squad victims. They are naked, like mutilated dolls.

In El Salvador, you have to choose sides; there is no middle way. Eventually, the sides will have to be brought together, but it is not going to happen without dramatic changes and sacrifice.

Adelberto

Adelberto, aged two, spends twelve hours a day in the San Salvador market. His mother, Blanca, is giving him a bath behind the racks of cheap polyester dresses. His baby sister, María Rosa, is asleep in a cardboard box. Two older brothers, aged five and seven, sell toys that clack and cost fifty cents each.

A typical market family. Their father, said Blanca, is "travelling." She has not seen him for a year. He might be back soon, but nobody knows for sure. Blanca makes so little, sometimes only a twenty-five-cent profit on four toy sales a day, if she is lucky.

Blanca Villatorio worked in the market before she was married and expects to work there for the rest of her life. The boys will work with her until they find better jobs. The baby will grow up to work until she, in turn, gets married — and will probably go on working even then. The market is their world. It is also their prison.

The International Labour Organization (ILO) in Geneva estimates that fifty million children around the world work so that their families can survive. In many countries, the child workforce is growing and school attendance is declining. In 1979, the Year of the Child, the ILO urged its 150 members to ratify a minimum-age convention that set fifteen as the lowest age for employment. But throughout the Third World children either work or they don't eat. Adelberto, too, will be working in another two years.

The market children in San Salvador overflow the sidewalks, shouting and jostling, part of the clamour that characterizes the Salvadoreans more than any other people in Central America. Pitch-men for the latest plastic watches use amplifiers to be heard above the shouts and the blaring buses. Women with baskets on their heads push through a running tide of squirming humanity. Instead of the embroidered *trajes* of Guatemala, the women of this city wear, as do the men, a riot of scarlet nylon and acid-green shirts, cheap sneakers in hot pink, and T-shirts with emblems ranging from Harvard University to the Toronto Seamen's Mission.

The market-sellers offer posters of Jesus Christ and Michael

Jackson and a chimpanzee on the toilet. They sell pornographic comics and Spanish fashion books, shoe laces, socks, roses, strawberries, and plastic Superman toys, all jumbled crazily together. I ask Blanca about school. Do the older boys go to classes? No room in the local school, she says, shrugging her shoulders, not a bit surprised. Then she adds another reason:

"I would like them to go to school, but see, they don't have shoes. And where would I get the money for books? It costs money to send your children to school. Maybe one day, when their father comes home."

It is hard, she admits, to keep an eye on Adelberto and on the baby while she works. Adelberto runs off if she turns her back for just one minute. Most of the time, she has to keep him in an upturned crate so that he stays put. But there is nothing she can do. There is nobody else to care for the children. At least the boys are earning a useful living and are getting good at arithmetic. "They never take a penny for themselves. They are honest boys."

A 1983 university study of 355 children working in San Salvador showed that eighty per cent of them had begun to work before they reached the age of ten; seven is the most common age. Most of them work at selling in the markets or on the streets. They work six or seven days a week, never less than five, and most often for eight hours a day. More than ninety per cent said they work because their parents need them to work, and eighty per cent give all the money they earn to their parents. More than half have intestinal infections and almost half have bronchial or lung problems. When they get sick, most parents resort to household remedies, saying the hospitals charge too much to take the child there, or that there were long line-ups. Most children (72.7 per cent) do not go to school now — and have never been to school. Whenever they do go, they are several grades behind the other kids. Anyway, with unemployment high and no jobs for teachers, or even doctors, many parents see no point at all in an education.

A two-page article in *La Prensa Gráfica* on September 30, 1984, bewailed the "shadows on the horizon for our children" and showed photographs of market kids, barefoot, working on shoe repairs. It cited the UNICEF publication, *The State of the World's Children*, but did not mention that infant mortality in El

Salvador is seventy-five per thousand, compared with nine per thousand in Canada.

El Salvador's education and health budgets have been cut every year since the civil war began in 1979. A price hike for staple foods, such as rice, and a wage freeze for most workers have made it even more difficult for women like Blanca to make ends meet.

So child labour is increasing. In 1975, only twelve per cent of children between ten and fourteen were working. The most recent survey, done by the government in 1979, showed sixteen per cent of them working. Carmen Ivette Bara, who surveyed child labour for the Centroamerican University in San Salvador, believes the figure has grown even higher in the 1980s. With per capita GNP (gross national product) at only $700 a year, the decision to put a child to work is not a free choice: "It is not irresponsibility or immaturity, lack of culture or education that puts them to work. It is the inevitable reality imposed by survival needs," she says.

The ILO recognizes that reality. "Given the low education or skill content of many of the jobs in which working children are involved, the possibilities of acquiring remunerative or satisfying skills become still more remote. Children thus find themselves locked in low-paying, unskilled, unpleasant and unsafe work conditions," said Francis Blanchard, the ILO director-general, in July 1984.

For Adelberto, though, the market is a second home; and for his brothers, it is an opportunity to contribute to the family income. The seven-year-old told me he wants to work for himself, as a salesman, when he grows up. Out in the streets, the shoeshine boys and the kids selling newspapers are frequently prey to the bigger boys or gangs of juvenile thieves. Close to their mother, Blanca's kids feel safe. It is hot and crowded in the market, but it is a friendly place.

In the Third World, one hundred million children work for a pittance; in another two or three years, Adelberto will join them.

Eva

Eva Eugenia is a success. She was recently crowned Miss Central America, and she is also vice-president of El Salvador's major drug company, Laboratorios López. Her dad is president. She is popular, rich, intelligent, beautiful, and totally untouched by the war that has turned El Salvador into the butcher's shop of the world.

Well, not quite untouched. She no longer has her six horses. And the old polo grounds have been ploughed up because so few officers now have time to play. Life is "more serious."

Eva Eugenia is in her early twenties (she refuses to be more specific), and would probably win my admiration if I interviewed her for a Canadian society page. Is it her fault that her success story seems indecent in El Salvador? Is it her fault that success has come so easily to the company-president's daughter?

Laboratorios López is one of a dozen fortress-like factories in the working-class suburb of Soyapango, famous for the number of bodies that regularly show up on the sidewalks at dawn after a busy night for the death squads. Huge walls, electronic gates, and armed guards control the entrance. On my first visit for a promised interview, I did not even get beyond the security guard. He had no notice of my arrival and made me return next day.

When I finally meet Eva Eugenia she is all apologies and graciousness. In a pearl-grey silk shirt and expensive grey-flannel pants, she extends a cool hand to me with elaborate formality. Her English is perfect; after all, she was educated at the American school in San Salvador and at Wellesley College, an all-women college in Boston, Massachusetts, where she studied economics and French. Further studies in Paris perfected her French, and almost led to her marrying a Frenchman.

I ask if she changed her mind and returned out of concern for her country. She is honest:

"It was more to please my family, and to get a chance to prove I could be as good at business as any man. You see, my brothers work in the family business, too. Salvadorean women are only just now beginning to be accepted in business, and it was my chance to prove something for other women, as well as for myself. Besides, my father wanted me back."

Eva Eugenia is in charge of traffic control. She monitors the

Eva Eugenia.

numbers of pills, the numbers of bottles, the packaging materials, and the orders. Graphs of figures are piled neatly in her in-tray on an almost bare desk. Surrealistic oil paintings on the wall behind her include one of anguished eyes and barbed wire. I ask if it has any connection with El Salvador.

"Oh no. It's by a French painter I know. All his stuff is very spiritual. I am not interested in realism in art."

In her high-tech office, furnished in chrome and leather and with at least a dozen pens in the holder on her desk, Eva Eugenia is out to impress me with her efficiency, and her accomplishments.

She has been valedictorian every year at school. She has won prizes in international exhibitions of flower arranging. She has acted as a host on TV. She has won national awards for equitation on her mare Roselana. She likes paintings and poetry, "quiet" jazz, and French literature, especially the nineteenth-century classics. She also loves the open air, and has even hunted boars in the forests outside Paris. "I am satisfied with what I have done. I feel I am living up to my own ambitions and to those of my family and my university. My mother always encouraged me to have a career. She never had one, so I suppose I am carrying out her ambitions. Some people might call me assertive. I don't think I am pushy or aggressive, but I am not a mild person."

Eva Eugenia is proud to tell me that all the forepersons in the factory are women. Women, she claims, are more reliable than men, "and less likely to be trouble-makers." There is no union in the factory, she said, "because we treat our women like one of the family and they know we value them. A union would put us against each other."

At this point she works only part-time. She is driven to the office in the chauffered family car at eight-thirty in the morning. She works a few hours, eats lunch at her desk, and afterwards is whisked off by the beauty contest organizers for public appearances and interviews. She will have to travel and she thinks it will be "something of a bore" but worth it because all the proceeds of the pageant in El Salvador go to help disabled soldiers. Eva Eugenia also does other "charity work," helping to organize concerts to raise money for the wounded soldiers.

The beauty contest itself has in no way awed Eva Eugenia. She is proud to report that the U.S. military attaché was one of the jurors. She shows me her album of colour photographs of herself, in a swimsuit, in a white ballgown that emphasizes her long neck, and in a costume she made herself out of Salvadorean cotton towels and necklaces of coffee beans, for the "traditional" sector of the contest.

"There really isn't a traditional native dress except plain white cotton, and that's not very exciting," she explains. I restrain myself from bringing up the fact that El Salvador has just about wiped out its native population. Many of them died in the 1932 massacres and the rest were so shell-shocked they dropped their Indian languages and customs. Now the 2.3 per cent of the population who admit to being Indian are totally ignored.

Eva Eugenia sees nothing wrong with beauty pageants, or with the lavish parties that go with them. "We have to live. I live an enjoyable life but I work hard. I don't read the newspapers very much. I never go out alone or downtown after dark. We have a private electricity plant at home, so we are not troubled by the black-outs.

"It is amazing how easily you can get used to the tragic effects of war. You even get used to seeing dead bodies in the streets. I try to do my best by raising money for the soldiers, to buy wheelchairs."

She blames her country's miseries on "subversion, Communism, and land reform, which led to the break-up of our traditional economy." She supported Roberto D'Aubuisson, the right-wing candidate in the 1984 elections, and is against the Christian Democrats because they are "soft on Communism."

"You only have to look at Nicaragua to see what a real mess the Sandinistas have made of that country. We don't want that to happen here.

"If you don't have a strong economy and authority, you get anarchy. We know that, but other countries are always trying to make us over in their own image."

I ask her what she thinks the challenge is today for the young people who are leaders of their society in El Salvador.

"They should be taking responsibility, the women as well as the men. There is no longer a place for rich young people who simply enjoy themselves."

She wants to work, even if she gets married. She is pretty sure she will marry, but not just yet. She might even live somewhere outside El Salvador. Why not? "It is not good to be restricted to one country."

Just before I had met Eva that afternoon, I had visited a refugee camp where several hundred women and children have been "restricted" to a church courtyard for the last three years. So, before I leave Laboratorios López, I ask her if she can give me any medicines, knowing that headache pills cost fourteen cents apiece. She takes me to meet her father, who gives me five bags of medicines for the refugees.

Later, I give one bag to the Families of the Disappeared. I take the other four to the FMLN guerrillas in Chalatenango.

Juan Antonio

Guerrillas, I thought, ought to look fierce. Juan Antonio would never get the part if this was Hollywood and not FDR/FMLN rebel territory in El Salvador. His moustache straggles. His uniform is jeans and a black wind-cheater. He is sitting in a café, playing with a baby and watching *The Incredible Hulk* on TV. But he never once sets down his M-16 gun.

It is eight in the evening, and I've just arrived in the little mountain town of La Palma, where the first dialogue between the Salvadorean authorities and the FDR/FMLN will take place in a few days' time. I travelled, with some trepidation, on the regular bus that passes between the government-held territory and the area under rebel control. Half-way through the trip, the checks by army troops ended. Further on, a polite FMLN guerrilla boarded the bus, read us the latest news from the rebel broadcast, Radio Venceremos, and passed the hat for those who would like to contribute; everybody on my bus did.

I was nervous on the bus, because I had four bags of medicine under my poncho, and also because I had never met a guerrilla, and couldn't quite extinguish my fears of men with guns, however much I might applaud their cause.

Juan Antonio and a dozen of his *compañeros* (*compas*, they call them) mingle with the locals. If it had not been for the guns, it would be impossible to tell who was who. Townsfolk and guerrillas have a football game fixed for next Saturday, according to the notice pinned to the café door. I pick out Juan Antonio to talk with because he is the man with the baby. The baby really belongs to the woman who runs the café, but it loves being clucked over by the men, who appear to miss family life; it is likely they'd rather be home with the kids than fighting.

Juan Antonio is solemn, almost sad. Only twenty years old, he joined the armed resistance when he was thirteen, and has been fighting ever since.

"I joined up with most of my friends in Grade Six because the death squads in Santa Ana, where I lived, were treating the peasants like animals, and I was very angry. They trucked peasants from the coffee to the cotton fields in cattle trucks, and made them work while aircraft sprayed the crops. They moved the cattle away to safety, but not the peasants.

Juan Antonio.

"My father died when he was forty-nine and my mother when she was fifty. They were old people, worn out with work and with looking after seven children. I was the oldest, and I am sorry I could not help them more. We were a typical *campesino* family, illiterate and always desperate for food. My family knew I had joined the armed resistance, but I could not keep in touch. That is one of the sad things about the people's army; you have to leave a normal life behind. If you don't have very strong convictions, that is hard."

After talking with him for more than an hour, I find out that Juan Antonio's companion, his *compañera*, was killed in August 1982, fighting alongside him. He still wears the tiny, beaded necklace she made for him.

"I am not sad when I think of her, because she had chosen this life, and she would want to have died as she did. It is just sad that she died so young, and that we had no children.

"I do not think I will ever have children, and that hurts me. I do not think, either, that I will live to the end of this fighting and know what it is like when the people run their own country and there is justice for everybody. Maybe I believe in fate. I am not obsessed with it, but I have this feeling I will not be alive very long."

If he was not fighting in what he calls "the people's army" (not the guerrillas), Juan Antonio would like to be a teacher. He likes the history lectures given to the soldiers. He knows a great deal about U.S. history — about Roosevelt and the New Deal, about the 1930 Depression, about farm subsidies, and the civil rights movement. He knows that Canada is part of the British Commonwealth, and thinks it is still governed by the Queen. At least, he says, Canada doesn't have to do what the United States says. The Canadian government isn't a "puppet," like the Salvadorean government led by José Napoleón Duarte.

I am curious about the daily life of a guerrilla, but I can't get much information from Juan Antonio. The food, he says, is "adequate." He sleeps in a hammock in camp, but on the ground when on manoeuvres. There's no such thing as regular hours, because they might be on the move for twenty-four hours at a time, with rest breaks.

Juan Antonio doesn't seem to have any personal possessions at all. The pocket radio he carries belongs to "all of us"; the water bottle is FMLN issue. So are the boots, "liberated" from the Salvadorean army.

His M-16 was also taken from the Salvadorean army; Juan Antonio has taken "many, many more." He confirms that new rebel recruits have to win their guns, though this is becoming easier because so many regular soldiers defect to the guerrillas, bringing their weapons with them. Later, the regular army's public relations officer admits to me that recruits inducted for their military service are given a battery of loyalty tests because it is suspected that young men intent on joining the rebel forces get their guns and training free from the army and then desert.

Juan Antonio seems sorry for the soldiers he is fighting. "It is not their fault. They have no choice, so they are victims. If they don't fight, the army shoots them. If they do fight, we shoot them." He is not so sympathetic to the pilots who bomb civilian villages. A-37 airplanes and helicopters use rockets and 250-pound bombs against defenceless people. There are also *verdugos*, executioners, among the Salvadorean army. Juan Antonio confirms a story I heard from the Legal Aid Office of the Catholic Archdiocese of San Salvador, about a search-and-destroy operation in Chalatenango, during August 1984. At least thirty-four unarmed peasants died, some of them drowning when they jumped into the Gualsinga River to try and escape the bullets.

"That is the very worst thing, when the old people and the children are killed. They did not choose to fight. We did. If a *compañero* is killed, we do not mourn. But it is so sad to see the burned bodies of old women or little kids.

"I think about my mother and father. I think about the kids I will never have."

Are you angry? I ask.

"When I am fighting, yes. But mostly I am sad."

What does he enjoy doing when he is off duty?

"What I am doing now, watching TV, playing with the local kids. Being in La Palma is like coming back to a real world for me. Except that the army comes here from time to time. They drive through. We don't want to fight them in a town where the people would get hurt, and they won't come after us because they know we are too strong for them. So mostly they leave us alone. Chalatenango is FMLN territory. We can sit around here, have coffee, go to church." Juan Antonio wears a small silver cross and says that although there is a priest with the guerrillas in Chalatenango, he has been to the church in La Palma. The church is called "The Sweet Name of Mary," and will be the site of the FDR/FMLN's meeting with Duarte.

How does a Catholic reconcile his religion with the necessity of killing?

"I believe what Monseñor Romero believed," he answers (Archbishop Oscar Arnulfo Romero was assassinated March 24, 1980). "He said the poor have a right to defend themselves against injustice when all other ways have failed. The poor have no guns, but we are their guns. And we, too, are the poor. Nobody pays us to fight. We accept it as our duty.

"But it still makes me sad."

Demetrio

All through the rains, Demetrio teaches his Grade Four students from under an umbrella. Their part of the room is pretty dry, but the ceiling above Demetrio leaks. The floor is so uneven that the kids keep tripping over it. There are no school books, no pencils, no exercise books, and only one precious stub of chalk for the board.

"It's a typical San Salvador school. I know worse," he comments. I find Demetrio Antonio Turcios Nuñez, aged twenty-four, along with five hundred other teachers on a one-day protest outside the Ministry of Education. Well-ordered and quiet, they have taken over the parking lot for "an educational" to make people aware of the problems for teachers and students in El Salvador.

"I'm fighting for myself, but I am also fighting for better conditions so that the children can learn," insists Demetrio. He is paid about $30 a week, but hasn't been paid since April. He says the same is true for hundreds of teachers. He has to teach a class at a private school and sell gold chains, watches, and rings as a sideline to pay the rent. "I'm supposed to be studying law, too. If anybody tells you we are a lazy people, they don't know Salvadoreans."

Demetrio, a stocky man with an unsuccessful beard, was born in La Unión, and has three brothers and six sisters. He went to a rural school, graduated as a teacher because he had aunts and uncles who taught, got married, and is now in charge of thirty-seven students at a mixed primary school in Soyapango, the industrial *barrio* of the capital.

He is about to become a father, and is worried about how he is going to pay the doctor. Back in 1978, he says, the government had agreed to provide medical treatment at reduced cost to teachers and public employees, but nothing has happened. He reckons it will cost him $500 for the birth and for his wife's stay in hospital. He has no savings at all.

"What annoys me is that the government has deducted two per cent from my salary every month for the last two years for a health program that doesn't exist. And now we hear that the government spent six million dollars of our money to send a soccer team to Spain. We didn't even win!"

Demetrio and his fellow members in the teachers' union, ANDES 21 de Junio, have plenty of complaints. Five thousand teachers are out of work, and two thousand schools throughout the country have been closed down. Two hundred and fifty thousand children do not go to school. Those who do go learn very little because of school conditions.

"I have had to tear up the pages from my student notebooks and hand them round to my class so they have something to write on. Lots of kids learn how to write on the chalkboard, but never once get to write on paper or to read from a book. It is just memory and board work.

"If we ask for even a football, we are told we'll have to buy it ourselves or ask the children to bring money. But we know they don't have money. As it is, some of them come to school without shoes."

Demetrio is angry, not so much over his own appalling work conditions, but for the children. He says the education budget has gone down over the past few years, while the defence budget has soared. Secondary school students are suspect by security forces just because they are young and therefore might be "subversives."

Teachers are the army's common targets. Executive members of the ANDES union have been murdered, its headquarters have been bombed and raided, and its members repeatedly threatened. But they are remarkably militant still. In 1983, ANDES arranged for the "best teacher" awards to go to the relatives of teachers who had been murdered, imprisoned, or had disappeared following arrest. The stony-faced Minister of Education had to hand out the awards at a public ceremony. But militancy has not gained ANDES many of its demands. Pensioned teachers still get only $25 a month. Qualified teachers get ranked so low that they are paid beginners' wages.

"We are fighting a common misconception about a teacher's role. In Latin America, tradition has it that the local teacher is thin, poor, and hungry. If anybody takes education seriously, this attitude must change. Instead, we are getting thinner, poorer, and hungrier," Demetrio complains.

He does not want his future child to be a teacher. "It is a dangerous job and it does not pay you enough to keep you alive. Better that he be a lawyer."

Many teachers have given up, believing that the government neglect of education has made their jobs impossible. In 1979, when the killings began to escalate, Minister of Education Salvador Samoya himself resigned, and went over to the guerrilla forces, saying: "Our education program is a farce. In El Salvador there is no childhood."

But Demetrio does not want to give up or join the armed struggle. He still feels that the only way to change society is through education, even if it is a slow process and the rewards are scarcely visible.

"I can understand people giving up," he tells me. "I see the children fighting in the street, imitating what they see on TV or in the movies, or else copying the police when they raid a home. I, too, wonder what has happened to the child in El Salvador.

"But I will stay. Maybe they need me, and I am happy when I teach. It is hard to do a double job, to try and study and worry where the money is coming from. But teaching is not a job you take up and put down. It is a vocation."

In 1979, according to UNICEF, the literacy rate in El Salvador was 68.5 per cent. But on November 20, 1984, the Salvadorean Minister of Education announced the necessity for a new literacy campaign because the literacy rate was only 40 per cent, the lowest rate in Central America. It had gone down 28.5 per cent, the result of closing down schools all over the country. In 1984, 22,736 children were unable to attend classes because of school closures, lack of money for teachers, and new "priorities."

Over the same period in Nicaragua, the literacy rate went up from 48 per cent to 87 per cent, because of the literacy crusade where 95,000 young people blanketed the country, teaching the young and the old, men and women, to read. Literacy was the first priority of the new Sandinista government. In El Salvador, no such premium has been placed on the value of literacy.

"We have become a country of idiots," comments Demetrio, "and I believe our government really wants us to be stupid, so that the people cannot find out for themselves or think for themselves. How can you have a democracy if you close down schools?"

Dalia

I pick out Dalia Navarrete from all the other dancers in the folklore ballet performing at San Salvador's National Theatre one Saturday afternoon. With enormous black eyes, wide smile, and long-braided hair, she has the slight body of a child: a lyrical, flexible body. Later I find out she is only fifteen.

I am at the theatre with about fifty other persons. We make a pathetically small audience in a crimson-plush and gilt theatre so dusty that it makes me cough. On the stage, the dancers are on their knees, "washing" clothes, imitating the daily chores of scrubbing and banging the washing on invisible rocks by the side of an invisible river.

The other dancers are enthusiastic and well-trained amateurs. Dalia is a real dancer, riveting the eyes of her audience, even when on her knees. She plays numerous roles: a young nun, a rich girl from the city, a five-year-old, bratty kid. Each time she's believable and a joy to watch.

During the intermission, I go backstage to talk with her and find out that Dalia has no hope of ever making dancing a career. "Nobody earns a living as a dancer in El Salvador," she says. "There is no dance company with paid dancers. We have to borrow money ourselves to rent this theatre, make costumes and props. It costs us a lot of money to dance. There is no government help, no help from the city, no help from anybody."

All the dancers are students. Their leader and choreographer, Roberto, teaches athletics and dancing at the university. He is paid by the students, not the university authorities who have no money for non-essentials.

Dalia doesn't know what she might do for a career. She would dearly like to be a doctor, but that, she says, is about as impossible as becoming a ballerina. She has five brothers, and they are more likely to get further education than she is.

The second half of the performance gives me another insight into Dalia. It is a dance created from children's games: jumping rope, jacks, Red Riding Hood, the little orphan, the bridge of Aragón, the donkey, the rat and the cat. I'm quite puzzled by it. It is a lot of fun to watch the dancers cavorting like kids, but why make it into a ballet? I ask Dalia when I meet her again after the show.

"You don't understand because, in your country, children play. Children in El Salvador don't play. They are too busy working. Or they don't have the energy, they suffer from malnutrition. Even the government admits that eighty-five per cent of our children suffer from malnutrition. Look at their swollen bellies. That comes from worms. Look how pale they are. They sit with their bare feet in the gutter, like little old men and women.

"That's why I would like to be a doctor, if only I could. But it may help, in a little way, to show people how children play, or how they once played, because so many of the children's games are now forgotten. Nobody seems to care.

"What I like best of all is to go out to Panchimalco, where there is still an Indian community. They have preserved a few of their dances, and we are learning from them so that we can show their dancing to other Salvadoreans. Hardly anybody has pride in our Indian heritage. We'd like to change that, in some little way."

Dalia has taken a year's classical ballet training, taking classes one evening each week, but she much prefers folk dancing: "I don't really want to do all the ballet exercises every day. What is the point? It is too remote from our lives."

But folk dancing, she explains, gives her a way to forget her own personal problems.

"When I dance I am not an individual. I represent a whole

Dalia Navarrete.

people. I am all the women at the saint's day celebration. I am all the young girls, flirting with the young men and running away. I am all the women who wash their clothes at the river, day after day.

"It is almost scary, that feeling. I feel I am part of all the births and deaths, the fiestas and the harvest, all the things that go on, year after year. I become much more than just me."

Dalia insists she has no interest in politics. She won't talk about the government, or about the war. Nobody talks about it at school, she says. And she doesn't read the papers. "Most of my friends know what is going on, but we don't discuss it. Maybe I would say the wrong thing, and I would get in trouble. We all feel that way, so we avoid it.

"I do think about it, though. When I bought a skipping rope

for the dance we just did, I tried it out in the street. I could just remember some of the rhymes we would say when we skipped, years ago.

"But the children on the street watched me as if I had brought in a toy from another country. That is sad, when children don't know how to play. They have a right to be happy. Children's games are part of our heritage. Our people are losing their roots, even their identity. There are so many thousands of displaced people, and so much misery that children are not children any more."

Elsa

Elsa, aged seven, is supposed to be having fun. She is one of a hundred kids from the Domus María refugee camp in San Salvador who have been led hand-in-hand to a children's party behind a local church. The neighbourhood kids fought and shouted, giggled and pushed each other around. The refugee kids, still holding hands, formed a ring on the outside, staring, silent. It is the official Day of the Child.

Elsa is glowering. Only the rounded cheeks and wistful mouth speak to the "child" she is. Her knit brows, accusing eyes, and set mouth would be more fitting on somebody older. Her black hair is uncombed, her sneakers are several sizes too large, and her dress is bright pink and home-made. Most of the refugees at Domus María wear clothes made from the same donated bright-pink cotton.

Elsa clutches at the fingers of her friend Margarita, whose belly is so rounded by worm infestation that she looks pregnant. They watch the other children play "cat and mouse," and "guess my name," and "all change." Then one of the boys climbs a tree to string up the *piñata* — a paper-maché donkey that will break and rain down candies once somebody, blindfolded, bangs it hard enough with a stick. When it does break, neither Elsa nor Margarita run for the candies. It is almost as if they know there isn't enough for everybody. They sit with the others for a sing-song, and some of the refugee kids join in, but not Elsa. When they leave, they link hands again in a line, making no

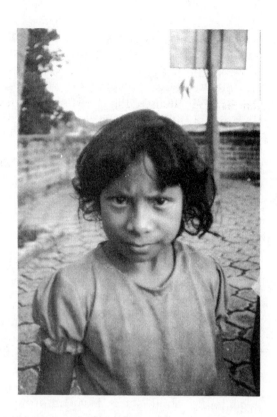

Elsa .

fuss. I follow them back to the camp.

There are 341 children under the age of fifteen in the yard at Domus María, along with 110 adults, most of them women. Some of them have lived there for four years, after fleeing from Chalatenango, San Vicente, La Libertad, or Cuscatlán because of the fighting. It looks like quite a nice camp, with wooden shelters for sleeping, a workroom with sewing machines, a storeroom for food, and a tin-roofed shelter for a schoolroom. I have seen other camps in San Salvador where all that refugees had for protection from the months of hard rain was a piece of torn plastic. I saw one camp where they lived in a basement, day in, day out.

The Archbishop's office provides food for the refugees, but there is only enough for 300, and 551 refugees have to eat. Medical supplies consist of four bottles of cough medicine, some aspirin, and a box of bandages. A doctor comes once a week. There are half a million displaced people in El Salvador. Half of them live in camps like Domus María, surviving on United Nations food aid and church hand-outs. They very rarely leave the camps, justifiably: they are too terrified. In 1983, three people were taken out of Domus María by the military; they disappeared. Police raided the medical supplies twice in 1984. Local people, except for the church, have their own problems and want nothing to do with refugees. Many suspect the refugees of being "subversives" because they have fled from the army.

When I ask the way to the camp, very few local people even know it exists. And very few adult refugees ever venture outside the guarded gate.

Diego and Aldano, two young men from the Human Rights Commission who have come to guide a discussion group, help me find Elsa again. She is sitting alone, tying and untying knots in a bit of string. Diego and Aldano have to help me because Elsa's Spanish is hard to understand and her voice very weak.

Elsa comes from San Vicente. She has been in Domus María three years, and can remember very little before that. Once she had "many" brothers, two sisters, a mother and father, and a grandmother and grandfather living with her in a *champa* (thatched-roof hut) in the countryside. They had a big black pig.

"The soldiers came. We all ran out of the house, down the road, to a gully. I hid in a little space behind a rock," she whispers. When she came out, a neighbour stopped her and would not let her go into her own house. She doesn't know why. The neighbour took her along with her own children, on the long walk to San Salvador. That was all she could remember.

I get the young men from the Commission to ask her if her parents were killed. "She says she doesn't know. She thinks somebody told her they were dead, but she has forgotten who it was."

"I don't remember" is the only answer I can get from her. She repeats it sing-song, her hands twisting the little piece of string.

Who looks after her in the camp? I ask. Diego and Aldano tell me the children are all fed, they go to lessons, they have clothes and shoes — at least most of them. But they look after themselves. They play in gangs. They don't respect the adults.

That appears to be true. The women and a few old men sit listlessly in the shade of the tin-roof, out-of-place *campesinos*, useless and unwanted, while the kids fight over bottlecaps or their one precious soccer ball. Could Elsa be adopted if she was an orphan? I ask.

"But maybe she isn't an orphan. Maybe her parents are in a refugee camp in Honduras or in Mexico, or maybe they are in FMLN zones. It is impossible to know for sure. She is one of thousands like this," replies Diego.

"There are kids here who saw their parents murdered, and who wake up screaming from nightmares, night after night. There are kids and women who were raped. Nobody knows what goes on in their minds now, or what will happen to them in the future. Are they going to live in a camp like this for the rest of their lives? Nobody knows. Nobody cares."

Later, I visit Sister Maritchi, a Belgian nun, herself an orphan, who now runs a home for older Salvadorean orphans down the road from Domus María. Forty orphans live with Sister Maritchi as a family — not as refugees, she insists.

"The kids who come to me have no papers, no family, no discipline, no love. They come to me like angry wolves."

Maritchi's plan is to give them a routine, responsibility, and high expectations. The boys get up at five in the morning, make breakfast, clean up, even sweep and wash the sidewalk, and get lunch ready for the girls, who have been in school all morning. Then the girls take over while the boys go to school. Right now, the boys are building an extension to allow for more dormitories, and the girls are embroidering flour sacks to sell as cushion covers in the market. The older children go to high school, and those older still are being trained for jobs. Several have stayed on at Maritchi's to help out, regarding the home as their family.

Maritchi's home survives on donations from Belgium. She knows how little she can do to help the tide of displaced, orphaned, and abandoned kids. "I can help a few, and with love and discipline they will make fine adults. But the rest will grow up like animals, unless the authorities take responsibility for these children. I fear that will never happen."

She sends me to the Bloom Children's Hospital, known as one of the best hospitals in the country, to see what things are like for the other children of El Salvador, those who aren't refugees. Rebecca Giral, chief of the social work office, sees my camera and says, "Come with me. See for yourself. Take pictures. People in El Salvador should know what is happening to their children." She is plainly angry.

In the hospital ward she shows me row upon row of children with swollen stomachs and twig legs. They are tiny, wizened: images more familiar out of Africa than Central America. In the most modern hospital in San Salvador, malnutrition is the number one disease.

"It is a vicious cycle. We don't cure children, we simply revive them so that they can go out and starve once more. Sometimes they get sick from simple infections that become serious for children without any resistance, children who don't get enough to eat. Three-quarters of Salvadorean children under five suffer from some grade of malnutrition.

"There is food in the country, but the poor cannot afford it. We have a twelve-year-old girl now, dying of malnutrition. Her father has a cow and chickens and grows beans and corn. He owes all of it to the man who owns his land, so his daughter and the rest of the family are starving. If he didn't hand over the milk, the eggs, and his crops, someone would come and take them, so what could the man do? It is a social and economic problem, not a medical one. We just bandage the wound; we don't cure anybody here."

Rebecca has worked at the Bloom Hospital for ten years. Each year, she says, the malnutrition cases get worse.

"I thought this would be a happy job, sending healthy children back to their mothers. Instead, every day I want to cry. If we cannot save the children, at the best hospital in El Salvador, who is going to save the children? Who?"

William Ramos

A student called William Ramos haunted my stay in San Salvador. "Freedom for William Ramos" demanded the scrawled writing on the wall beside my hotel. It was signed AGEUS, the university students' union.

81

"Freedom for William Ramos" — slogan painted by fellow students
on the walls of San Salvador.

Through the Human Rights Commission, I learned that William Ramos was an AGEUS leader, a medical student, who had
been arrested August 9, 1984, at 4:30 p.m. by armed civilians
outside the National Theatre. Members of the National Police
looked on but refused to interfere. After seven days of torture
in an unknown house, William Ramos was taken, still without
any charges against him, to the Mariona Penitentiary, where some
500 political prisoners are locked up. They have their own
organization in jail, and through them I found out that William
Ramos was still alive.

For three weeks I haunted the Ministry of Justice, trying to
get permission to see him, but without success. Next best, I
thought, would be to talk to his colleagues at the National University. Four years ago the army seized the campus, killing twenty-
nine students and workers. The previous rector was murdered.
For four years the university continued to operate using rented
rooms all over the city. But now, after international pressure,
the buildings have been returned to the university. It should be
easy, I thought, to find the students' union.

But the union building was just a pile of rubble. So were

the cafeteria, the laboratories, and the library. I watched work-men shovelling piles of burned books. Later, Dr. Miguel Angel Parada told me the soldiers had not only burned the books, they had even defecated on them. Science laboratories were noth-ing more than piles of twisted metal. Windows were out. Type-writers, radios, and equipment were carried away and sold. It looked like a Nazi occupation: a blitz against learning and culture.

Now, students are working on repairs; power lines and tele-phones have been reinstalled, ready for the new semester. The new rector sits in front of a portrait slashed by bayonets, while he arranges for me to pass a message to AGEUS, carefully avoid-ing official recognition of their activities. On my next visit, two AGEUS leaders waylay me, wanting to talk, but somewhere safe. We find a spare office; they check the windows and a friend stands guard at the door.

Their names are Luis and Julio, and I promise not to take their photographs. Slight and nervous, they are both unsure of me, but anxious for a chance to tell their story. I tell them I had seen the "Freedom for William Ramos" writing on the wall, and am curious. They nudge each other, embarrassed.

"We did it," they admit. "We did about twenty walls. The only time to do it is just after dark, when the police change patrols. It is too easy to get caught with a spray can alone in the street late at night. And that would probably be the end of you." That is Julio speaking, the journalism student.

They confirm the story about William Ramos. He is mar-ried, had a job — like forty per cent of Salvadorean university students — and still found time from his medical studies to work for AGEUS. He wasn't the last student to be picked up. And it is not only students who have been sought out; professors and university workers have fared no better.

Two days before our interview, a woman student was kid-napped from the parking lot of the law faculty; the cleaner who ran to stop the kidnapping was shot in the arm. The same week, a professor at the Catholic University was killed in front of his house. He was holding his two-year-old daughter in his arms when he got out of his car; a man with a G-3 rifle shot him twice in the face. The following week, the bookstore which the same professor ran downtown was set on fire.

Death-squad terror against students and intellectuals seems

like madness to me. I don't understand why those in power suspect those who read or teach. Julio advises me to remember Hitler: "Dictatorships thrive on ignorance. They fear anybody who questions.... AGEUS is simply a student organization. It has nothing to do with the FMLN armed opposition. But the army took over the university four years ago, killing twenty-nine people. And they have only handed it back because of international pressure.

"Just to be a student is dangerous in El Salvador. To be a student organizer is doubly dangerous."

The eight leaders of AGEUS have received telephone threats from the Anti-Communist Secret Army. They never go anywhere alone. They would like to open a legitimate office for the students' union on the campus again, but they are too nervous about attacks. It is hard enough for most students simply to attend university, to be threatened as well would make it too hard. They've decided it is better to continue in semi-clandestinity for the moment.

I ask about student life on campus. They tell me that most students came for classes at night, after work. Fees at the National University are low, only about $300 a year. At one of the twenty-seven private universities that sprang up, with government encouragement, when the National University was off campus, fees are $1,000 a year. According to the university's rector, Dr. Miguel Angel Parada, instruction in these "mushroom" universities is so poor that their students are rarely accepted by other institutions or able to start careers. They've been deceived by fancy brochures.

Posters for a concert, a dance, and a soccer game on the field close to the rector's office indicate there is a lighter side to life on campus. I talk to engineering students waiting for classes; they are upset about exam results and the price of computers. I ask them about AGEUS. They look at each other, pick up their books and tell me, politely, that they can't help me.

The same happens when I question medical students about William Ramos, the kidnapped medical student who was on the AGEUS executive. He isn't around any more. That's all anybody will say.

The AGEUS symbol is a head of Minerva, Greek goddess of wisdom. She is gagged.

Marta

Marta Peña, aged twenty-two, named her daughter Lidice after the Czech village where the Nazis murdered all the children.

"Does that sound sad?" Marta asks. "I don't want it to be a burden for her. I want it to be a name of hope, something nobody can kill. But you can't hope if you don't remember. That's why I called her Lidice."

But surely there are so many Salvadoreans who have been murdered. Why not name her after one of them? I ask. "That would be dangerous," Marta says. "That would be asking for trouble."

Marta looks like a schoolgirl. She's wearing a white blouse, no make-up, and her hair is pushed back from her ears. But she is no schoolgirl. She has a four-year-old daughter who goes to kindergarten and is cared for after school by Marta's mother. Her husband is a factory worker.

Marta works all day at the office of the Oscar Arnulfo Romero Committee of the Families of the Disappeared. Her brother, Waldo Edvidio, disappeared on August 7, 1981, when he was on his way to work at a clinic in Santa Ana. A white truck stopped, men with guns got out, picked him up, and he was never seen again.

"For two years, my mother and I were too scared to do anything. We went from the National Police to the National Guard. We went to the Rural Police, the Treasury Police, and the army headquarters. Nobody would admit my brother had been arrested or was in their power. My father is just a factory worker. We had no influence, we could do nothing. I was studying accounting, hoping to get a good job. But then my mother came to the office of the 'mothers,' as we call them here, and I came with her one day to see what they were doing.

"Now I work here every day, either in the office, or else I go around with food donations to the families of the disappeared who have so little to eat."

Working for the "mothers" is dangerous work in El Salvador. In 1983 Marianela García Villas, the committee's president, was killed while collecting proof that phosphorous bombs were being used against unarmed peasants. Some say she was tortured before being killed. Nobody was allowed to examine her

Marta Peña.

body, so nobody knows for sure. But the ample evidence of torture inflicted on other members of the "mothers" leaves little doubt about Marianela's treatment.

I've already seen the scars of this terror. At the committee's office one woman showed me the mess made of her abdomen and breasts by a machete. She was trying to find her missing husband and had gone to the police. At first they ignored her — "more important matters here, lady" — and then laughed at her — "so your husband has gone, who cares? Probably with another woman, good for him, or joined the communists, bad man, it's good for you he's gone." When she would not go away, continued to persist, they took her to a room and started to grill her. Eventually — as if in an unbelievable nightmare — they set about her with machetes. When they'd finished, they dumped her in a ditch, thinking she was dead. She wasn't. She had enough strength to crawl along the road until she found a peasant's hut. There she was given shelter and medical help.

Dozens of the "mothers" have experienced such reprisals for the sin of protesting the disappearance of their loved ones. I was told about María, who had been held in the custody of the National Police for fifteen days. Twenty men took advantage of her imprisonment by raping her and burning her with cigarettes. I heard of another woman, raped in front of her four young children. When they threatened to rape her oldest girl, aged only eleven, she begged them to do whatever they wanted with her but to leave her daughter alone. So they pushed the point of a rifle into her vagina. These are only three brief stories out of dozens I heard: stories that left me shaky and nauseous with shock. How do these women cope?

Sitting with Marta in the one quiet corner of the crowded office, above a pizza parlour on a busy San Salvador street, I ask her about the fear that seems to be everywhere, a constant in their lives. A spy-hole through the upstairs door lets the woman on guard-duty screen all visitors. The police are always present, sometimes in uniform, sometimes not, closely watching who comes and goes from the building.

"We're not very different from other people," replies Marta. "Everybody in El Salvador lives in fear. If you let it bother you, you would never get any work done."

Marta gets up at five a.m. every day, and gets home at seven p.m. She is usually in bed by ten. She hasn't been to a movie for two years. She had to quit her studies in accounting because her family received death threats, and she suspected there was an informer in her class at school. Her work with the disappeared is her life now.

"Anyway, I probably wouldn't have got a job even if I had finished my accounting. There aren't any jobs in El Salvador. And if you do get an offer of a job, you have to get a certificate from the police saying you are a respectable citizen. A lot of people in this committee have been denied their certificates.

"It means that this work has become my work, and the people here are my friends. I don't have any others."

Marta's committee began in 1977 when the disappearances started. Since then, more than five thousand Salvadoreans have

Adelberto.

disappeared following arrest, and more than fifty thousand have been murdered. Although an amnesty for political prisoners was declared in 1983, and some four hundred prisoners released, the prisons were full again within a few months. According to Marta, there are forty-five male teenagers in Mariona penitentiary, and another ten girls in Ilopango women's jail — just a few of the five hundred or so political prisoners. Some children live in jail with their mothers. In 1984, murders by the death squads dropped, but by then there were fewer dissidents left to murder. In the mid-1980s the number of disappearances is beginning to climb again. There is no evidence that a newly-appointed commission to investigate human rights violations will take its job seriously.

On the twenty-fourth day of every month, the "mothers" stage a protest. At first they sat down on the steps of the San Salvador Cathedral, but the police started to wait for them and make them move off. Now they usually go to a different church each month. "The best protests we have are those in the market, downtown," Marta says. "The market women support us and understand us. They hide our banners for us under all the bananas. We have had as many as three hundred people in one demonstration, and we've always managed to disperse before the police move in."

Marta never goes anywhere alone. She goes home with one of the other workers, and she never opens the door at night. How does this tension affect her trust in others, and in a better future? I ask.

"It has made me very cautious. I'm always hesitant before I talk to anybody. I try not to close myself off, because I think that is a bad example for Lidice. But she has to grow up to be cautious too or she won't survive. We women have a lot of fun together, here in the office; outside, we're withdrawn."

Does this fear make her bitter? Does she want revenge?

Marta clearly isn't happy with that word *venganza*. In El Salvador it smacks of gun-fights and lawlessness, and nobody could appear more gentle than Marta. She hesitates, and instead of answering tells me about a woman who had come to her for help the previous day.

"Her son was missing. Nobody would give her any information. And her son was a seventeen-year-old soldier in the Salvadorean army. We're all suffering, all the people of El Salvador. I wouldn't know who to accuse."

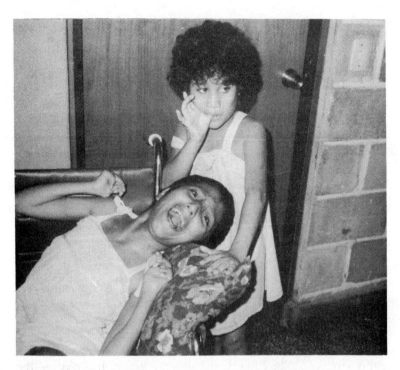

(*Above*) A deaf child tries to comfort her screaming friend in the
S.O.S. home for the children nobody wants. (*Below*) Acting out the
class struggle through the Pied Piper fable in Eduardo Bahr's class
in Tegucigalpa, Honduras.

■
Part Three

HONDURAS

HONDURAS, the unknown country. That is a journalists' label, and it covers up a lack of both knowledge and editorial interest in that bulge on the Atlantic side of Central America. Its capital has a name nobody can pronounce and a dinky little airport — a precarious strip of flat land boxed in between mountains — that gives you the willies when you fly into it. It is a three-day country. Visitors rarely stay longer. There are a few Nicaraguan "contras," and the U.S. troops, of course.

But don't bother with the Hondurans! Even the volcanos in Honduras are dormant! Such are the ways I've been warned against staying too long in Honduras. Such are the presumptuous opinions of those seeking an exotic vacationland. With equal presumption, I intended to defy all warnings and stay six weeks. I wanted to discover the national identity. It didn't help much when I landed at Tegucigalpa and found that the only national T-shirt on sale had the following message printed on it, in English: *"Where the hell is Honduras?"*

Well, if there was no national consciousness, I was determined to find out why not. Maybe I would find peaceful feudalism, an indication of what Central America was like before the Nicaraguan and El Salvador revolutions erupted. Maybe there would be sun-brown children playing in slumbering villages just like they do in the *National Geographic* magazine. Honduras, without a revolution, would be a welcome alternative to the horrors of violence. At least the children would not be suffering. So ran my first thoughts on arrival. I could not have been more wrong. Honduras emanates failure and indifference. The children are even hungrier than in the rest of Central America; they die just as surely. But in Honduras nobody seems to care. Nobody believes that Honduras can change, so nobody bothers to try. Instead of the picturesque underdevelopment of my fantasies I find the country is, rather, a classic case of over-exploitation. So exploited, in fact, that Hondurans take no responsibility for the mess and seem to have no ambition to improve things.

It would be easy to dismiss Honduras; easy to deride its politicians as incompetents, its guerrillas as bunglers, its generals as coxcombs, its citizens as shuffling *campesinos*. But Honduras did not choose its B-movie status, and its people deserve better.

Christopher Columbus was so glad to land on Honduras he named it after the *honduras* or "watery depths" he had escaped as he rounded the Gracias a Dios cape. There was talk of so much gold that it was rumoured the Indians used gold weights to hold down their fishing nets. But the difficult mountainous terrain and the lack of Indians to work the mines soon quenched enthusiasm. The country got tacked on to the Captaincy General of Guatemala and sank into neglect, disturbed only by Indian rebellions.

Few settlers arrived. Here, even the Catholic church was poor. Honduras had no public schools until 1784, a time when Guatemala and El Salvador already had universities. In spite of silver mines and a growing cattle industry, Honduras never developed a powerful upper class, let alone a middle class. It was a Honduran, Francisco Morazán, who united the Central American states after their independence from Spain. Morazán was shot in Costa Rica in 1842 by anti-unionist forces encouraged by the British ambassador. The British saw Morazán as a threat to their colonial efforts to the north in British Honduras, now Belize.

Since then, Honduras has known 262 civil wars, 48 wars with neighbouring countries, 13 different political constitutions, and 158 changes of government. It is one of the most unstable countries in Latin America, second only to Bolivia. This continual bickering and bloodshed prevented much development of either industry or large-scale agriculture. There were no fortunes made in coffee, as in Costa Rica, Guatemala, and El Salvador. No money poured into the nation's treasury for public works like roads. When U.S. mining interests arrived to re-open the silver mines, they were offered incredibly easy terms. The same went for the banana companies that arrived early in the twentieth century. The terms were so easy that in 1929, for instance, the United Fruit Company exported thirty-eight million bunches of bananas and paid Honduras just one penny per bunch.

The U.S. companies promised to build Honduras a railroad, and did so — but the lines ran only from the banana plantations to the ports, leaving Tegucigalpa as the only Central American capital without rail access. The banana companies monopolized electricity generation and use, the telephone service, the labour force, and the economy. They made and broke presidents. Their English became the language to speak. And when the banana lands were exhausted, the companies moved on, leaving behind only unemployment and desolation.

In Tela, the jungle has now grown over the white bungalows where American bosses used to call the "boy" for more whisky and soda. The streets of the city swarm with kids whose fathers no longer have work; these fathers are some of the twenty-two thousand who used to work for United Fruit, Standard Foods, and Cuyamel. The whole of the Honduran north coast resembles an abandoned company town. And Honduras has not been able to build on the rubble or create its own economy. It is still the poorest country in Central America.

Every day, forty Honduran children die from malnutrition or from childhood diseases that could be prevented, such as measles and whooping cough. More than half the population have never turned on a light or used a faucet. Infant mortality stands at 118 per thousand. Almost three-quarters of the population suffer from malnutrition, and for the poorest forty-two per cent, a daily diet provides only one-sixth of the calories and proteins they should be getting.

The trouble in Honduras is not shortage of land. The country is as large as England, and is the second-largest country in Central America. It has only 32 people per square kilometre compared with 212 in El Salvador. The problem lies in the ownership and use of land. Most agricultural land is owned by agribusiness companies to grow such export crops as bananas and pineapples. Foods like corn, wheat, and soybeans have to be imported at prices hardly anyone can afford. Most peasants cannot grow enough to keep their families alive because they don't have any land, or have too little.

While I was there, forty-eight workers were camping out, on hunger strike, in the central plaza of Tegucigalpa. The beggar children ran in and out of clumps of new arrivals who had just got off the bus to try and find work and a home in a city of slums. In El Aguacate, Olancho, two peasants died of starvation in October 1984; their homes and crops had been destroyed by U.S. troops building a military base.

In Comayuagua, the former capital of Honduras and now the local "good time" town for U.S. troops at the nearby Palmerola base, five houses of prostitution have sprung up since the Americans arrived.

Bessie, an eighteen-year-old prostitute with two gold front teeth (very much a status symbol), makes $200 on a good Saturday night, she told me — as much as many Hondurans make in one year. The U.S. medics at the sixty-bed military hospital spend much of their time running VD clinics for the women they call "business ladies." American military "aid" is having its usual effect.

But the more long-term effect of militarization by the U.S. is that Hondurans have again turned to the United States to make decisions for them. Every day the U.S. ambassador could be seen in consultation with the Honduran government, while his wife appeared on social pages, distributing food packages or school books.

"The tragedy of Honduras is that the errors of foreign exploitation over the last century have not been learned. They are being repeated once more," I was told by Efraín Días Arrivillaga, who in 1984 was the only Christian Democrat member of Congress.

There are causes for indignation everywhere: starving children, scandals over international aid, torture by the police, even plots by businessmen and generals to kill the Honduran president. Doesn't anybody care?

"If your stomach is empty, you tend to be concerned with your own needs. Indignation takes energy. Many people in Honduras are too malnourished to protest," a Jesuit priest told me. "What makes me marvel is that they don't resort to violence, that they do support each other, that human qualities prevail at all."

As I talked to the children, I began to learn what he meant.

Verónica

Verónica, aged eight, is a businesswoman. She sells newspapers twelve hours a day in the central plaza of Tegucigalpa. She keeps three cents for each newspaper and sells fifty to a hundred a day. On good days she earns three dollars — a worker's wage. She is proud of being a worker. "I don't like the kids who beg," she tells me, scowling. "I'm not like that. I am a *mujer de negocio* [literally, a businesswoman]." And she is. Verónica is much smarter at change than most adults and, of course, much better than me, a dumb foreigner. When I gave her the wrong coin, she shook her head sadly and corrected me.

Verónica's mother sells tortillas in the market. She brings Verónica to the plaza each morning at six, when a man on a bike dumps the pile of four different dailies on the sidewalk. Then she leaves Verónica on her little stool, after giving her a tortilla for her lunch, and walks three blocks to the market. Verónica is wearing warm pants under her check dress, and a cardigan pinned fast with a safety pin. She has good sneakers, too, but no socks. By local standards, she is a well-dressed child. Her long hair is well brushed and her face is always clean.

Her mother won't get back from the market until six p.m., but Verónica is watched over by dozens of vendors and loungers in the plaza. The kids hawk balloons, the adults, lottery tickets. The square used to provide work for shoeshine boys, but times have become so tough in Tegucigalpa that the men have taken over shoeshining. They have formed their own union, and chase the boys off. They now make do on the steps outside the main hotels, or outside the city's barber shops.

Everybody seems to know Verónica, and she is not afraid of being alone with her pile of coins. Verónica has one brother who works on the buses as a helper — he is the kid who helps passengers get off and on, collects tickets, and finds room for the baskets of vegetables, even a chicken or two. Another brother goes to school.

Verónica has never been to school. She cannot read the newspapers she sells. Her mother is not very concerned about school for her daughter: "She's smart, isn't she? She can add up faster than most teachers."

It is obvious that Verónica is loved and valued. While it might seem wrong for her to be working at age eight, she doesn't fit the image of an exploited child. In fact, she is doing better than most of the kids I meet. Verónica's family lives in Comayagüela, across the river, in a two-bedroom apartment with a kitchen and running water. I ask her about her father, and she says he went away several years ago. I soon discover that many Honduran fathers tend to disappear. Marriages are not regarded as permanent and many women have the responsibility of feeding the family.

A young mother with two small children is selling dried flowers in the shopping mall. A coin rolls out of her hand and down a drain. Digging desperately through the grating, she bites her lower lip, trying not to cry, doing everything possible to get that coin back. It is worth about ten cents. Just a few cents makes all the difference between surviving and going into debt.

The beggar children spend hours trying to fish up lost coins. They dodge in and out of the cafés, are shooed away and return, grab shoppers, even pinch your arm to get money. Sympathetic diners feed them from their plates before the manager can interfere. One ragged little girl, called Telma, pinches my wrist while I drink a cup of coffee. "Give me ten cents. Give me!" she hisses.

Walking through the square to get a bus at five o'clock the next morning, I can see where some of these children live —in cardboard boxes, without blankets, lying on the ground, with a newspaper underneath them if they are lucky. One boy is squished into a box marked "Very Dry Sherry from California." It is turned over on top of him against the thin rain, but his bare feet stick out. It is cold enough for me to shiver in a sweater.

Verónica's mother is worried about what will happen to her daughter when she turns twelve and is old enough to be prey for the gangs of boys who roam the streets. They are known to fight battles down by the river and rape the girls they cannot buy for a few cigarettes. Maybe, she tells me, it would be better for Verónica to work as a domestic in a "good" house, where she would not be at risk. But then, of course, the señor of the house, and his sons, often take advantage of servant girls.

"You see, it is hard to be a woman in Honduras," she sighs. "And we cannot protect our children as we would wish to do."

The plight of children is, indeed, a horror, not just because

Verónica.

of the statistics but because of the hypocrisy. In *La Prensa* news-paper, right beside the pious statement "We believe in the chil-dren of Honduras," runs another headline reading, "One teacher for eighty-nine children."

During my stay, two scandals provoked indignation, but nei-ther led to any real investigation or certainty that they would not happen again. The first concerned "fattening farms" run by lawyers who arranged adoptions of Honduran children by U.S. couples. The lawyers, and in one case a justice of the peace, bought the children from penniless young mothers, sent them to a home to be fattened up, and then fixed the adoption papers — for a fee. I met couples who had spent $12,000 for their babies, including lawyer's fees and paying for the waiting period for seeing the adoption through.

"The traffic in children has become a blasphemy against Jesus of Nazareth," thundered an editorial. But a couple of resignations did not stop the practice of selling kids.

The other scandal concerned the torturing of a ten-year-old boy by the investigations branch of the police, the DNI. Anselmo Ortíz Ramírez testified that his son had been arrested on a theft charge, held twenty-four hours, and then returned. The boy told his father he had been tortured with electric shocks. The police insisted the boy had "problems of malnutrition and psychic distress" and had not been tortured. But the doctor who examined him corroborated the charge. For two days, human rights advocates demanded an investigation, which, of course, never came.

There have been so many other scandals, from the theft of UNICEF milk donations to the disappearance of half a million dollars in the literacy campaign funds. "In Honduras, a scandal lasts two days and dies," I was told.

James P. Grant, executive secretary of UNICEF, visited Honduras in November, 1984, and concluded that the country had the highest infant mortality rate in Central America. Of the 800,000 children born each year, 90,000 die before they reach age five, and one of every ten that survives is too damaged to live normally. Half those deaths, Grant said, could be prevented. UNICEF proposed that the Honduran government spend more money to encourage breast-feeding, immunization, and oral rehydration programs. Government response was lukewarm.

I visited children's villages run by the S.O.S. Foundation, which relies mainly on international aid. Sister María Rosa, the S.O.S. founder, has built forty children's villages. But the hospital ward for handicapped children just outside Tegucigalpa remains an unaided dumping ground for quadraplegics, epileptics, the blind, the deaf, and the otherwise physically handicapped.

Nobody seems to care. There is no other residential home for these people, no government program. In Honduras, children are just not important.

The Honduran poet, Roberto Sosa, has written a poem called "The City of Begging Children." It was the sharpest voice of indignation that I heard:

Where do they come from, these begging children
and what forces multiply their rags?

Is there anyone who has not felt
deep in the heart
those sharp little fingers
of money-hungry birds?

Who has not stopped
to look at the bones of them,
hearing their voices like humble bells?

Let there be no more begging children
standing small in the doorways,
beaten by the fog of the cemeteries,
the white wall of the cities.

Let there be children with toys, and bread,
and stars beneath their shoes.

Let them be at school,
happily capturing insects on the lawn.

Let them live in their own world
among their own kind and their own things.[11]

David

At age seven David Funes is already a first-class con man. He is
sitting back in an armchair with an open newspaper, turning
the pages thoughtfully. I know he cannot read a word, but I
don't let on. He is such a great pretender.

For two years, David has been bringing in five dollars a day,
from begging on the buses — well over the average wage in Honduras. Some days he makes ten dollars. Having a crippled leg
helps, but David's charm helps much more. While talking to
him in the Dom Bosco Home for Working Children in Tela, an

[11] Roberto Sosa, "The City of Begging Children," translated by Alison
Acker from *Los Pobres* (Tegucigalpa, Honduras: Guaymuras S.A., 1983).

old banana port on the Atlantic coast, I find it hard to focus on the horror of his situation, he is so cute.

David's hair is cropped short because he has just come out of prison. They locked him up because he was part of a burglary gang. Once inside, he got the same treatment as everybody else. The police have a file on him that includes theft of a gun. Once out, he simply appeared at the Dom Bosco Home, saying he had heard they had a home for boys, he was a boy, so could he please come in? And, of course, he could. David's blend of pathos and shrewdness works, every time.

Jay, the Centre's U.S. volunteer, fills in some of the gaps in David's history for me, but admits he is never quite sure what is true and what isn't.

"He broke a leg as a small child, that is sure. Evidently it was not properly set, so he had to go about on crutches. His parents obviously took advantage of this to send him out, begging, and he did real well at it. For a time, he was working the buses between Tela and La Ceiba, making up to ten dollars a day. We think, though, that he didn't have money one night when it was time to go home, and so his parents didn't let him in. He doesn't know now where they are and we don't know either. He stays in the home, here.

"But grown-up men keep coming to call for him, to 'borrow' him. We found out that David had been taken up by a gang of burglars. Because he was so small he used to slip into a store, when it was getting dark just before closing time, and hide. Then, when the store-keeper had gone home, he would open up the door and let in his friends. It must have been quite an adventure.

"He's a bright kid, though he has never been to school and he can't read or write. The first day he was with me, he learned a few words in English, and he worked out how to spell them. He 'reads' the paper, though I don't know what he gets out of it. He's a funny mixture, very conceited, very manipulative, but very sweet.

"Sometimes he can be violent if he doesn't get his own way. He has learned that on the street. He has had to survive in an adult world, and goodness knows what experiences he has had."

David is waiting to be sent to a hospital in the United States. He has come to the attention of the Heal the Children program that takes such kids and returns them, cured. Doctors have said that proper setting of his fractured leg could make him walk straight once more. He will go with Jay. Maybe he will even go to Disneyland.

David lives in a house called "My happy little home." He loves playing with the dog or the two kittens. He has been to Tegucigalpa for the Games for the Handicapped where he won a bronze medal at frisbee.

He is one of the lucky kids at Dom Bosco. Many boys cannot live in the centre because they have to support their families. They push market-wagons, sell gum, clean boots, or steal. The Centre provides showers, hot meals, books, medical care, games, and a sympathetic ear, but does not try to run the kids' lives for them. They go on trips, even learn how to snorkel on the coral reefs off shore. They keep bees, hoping to make money on the project. They learn wood-working. But they are still street kids.

"They are used to staying out all night, sleeping on the beach, roaming all over town. They are not like other kids."

I ask Jay, in my ignorance, how the parents feel about having their kids in Dom Bosco. Didn't they miss their kids?

"Sure. Some of the parents miss the money. There is a lot of child exploitation in Honduras. The parents live off the kids. It's not as cosy as you imagine."

Jay tells me the story of María, aged four. Jay saw her in Tela, leading around her dishevelled mother, who mumbled and spat at strangers and scrabbled for food in the garbage. Her mother had a wound on her leg, and was treating it by rubbing it with ashes. María, wearing nothing but bloomers, kept her out of trouble.

"I saw her pull her mother by the hair to get her away from the traffic," Jay says. "That little girl smoked and drank. She ate cigarette butts. She was violent. Her mother hit her and she hit her mother.

"We couldn't get her into the home without getting treatment for her mother. Eventually we were able to get her mother a place in a mental hospital. Now we can do something for María, but it is going to take years. She's not the average four-year-old."

The kids he sees have skin diseases and venereal diseases and lice. They have never brushed their teeth, they are not used to washing or to eating at a table. All their young lives they have

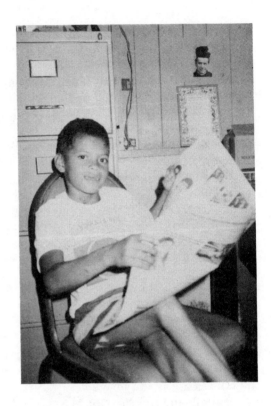

David Funes.

cadged and survived as best they could. Dom Bosco offers a chance at a different life. Parents are encouraged to take an interest and come to meetings to talk about their kids. But they don't have to come, and most of them don't. Some parents are hostile, most say they are too busy.

"The kids like puzzles and games," Jay says. "We play multiplication bingo. But they don't have the sort of imagination we expect children to have — the dreams of horses and clouds and trees and birds. They dream of being chased by the police or beaten by their dad. But they have their own kind of intelligence. They know how to manipulate people and how to survive. That will stand them in good stead for their adult lives. But they need time, too, to learn how to be children, to have fun on the beach, to tease and play. We take them into the forests and down to the beach as much as possible to give them this sort of life."

What will happen to David? I ask.

"He may turn into a very bright boy if he likes school and learns how to control his temper. And then, with a skill, he will do well. Right now, there are three Davids. One is a cute little angel — see that smile. Another is a little devil that you can't trust one minute or turn your back on. The third David is a scared little kid, who has never been allowed to be a child. Put them all together, and love him a lot, and he should make it. We only hope so, because there are thousands of kids like him in Honduras who won't."

Tito

Unripe bananas give you stomach-ache. Tito should know, because he eats them a lot when there is nothing else to eat, and that happens often. On good days, there are beans and corn tortillas. Some days there are just tortillas. And sometimes there is nothing at all. So kids like Tito grub around for whatever roots or fruit they can find.

Yet Tito lives on what we might call a farm. His family has a *milpa*, all two acres of it, with a patch of corn and a goat and a few chickens.

"The goat is no good. She has no milk. She's sick," Tito tells me. And eggs? "Mama sells them in the market."

He is a skinny kid, just eight years old. His T-shirt is torn and he has dirty shorts, knobbly knees, and no shoes. It is difficult to see him at all because he's hidden under an enormous load of firewood carried on his shoulder. I met him trudging along the highway twenty kilometres from Progreso, in the heart of the banana lands. Tito has a machete, too, wrapped in a rag, under the firewood. He uses it to cut the wood himself. He has to walk "a long way" to get it, and a long way to get home. His thatched-roof home is indeed a long way — four kilometres — from the stand of trees. The trees are private property.

In a country where pine forests abound and mahogany, rosewood, Spanish cedar, and balsa are national riches, there is no wood to gather for a fire. As well, there is no land for Tito's family, in a country with 112,088 square kilometres of land, and only thirty-two people on each square kilometre. The land belongs to either the sugar plantation owners and the banana company or the cattle ranchers. Families like Tito's get the leavings. Their two acres are rented. As rent they hand over most of the corn they grow. During bad years, they often go in debt because there's not enough corn to pay the rent.

Tito lives in a little village outside Progreso, inland from the north coast of Honduras. This area has long been a centre of rebellion by peasant groups enraged by the landowners. Up the road, at El Bálsamo, I saw the four graves of local men who were shot down by one of the many private police forces when they tried to take possession of land involved in a legal dispute. That was in the summer of 1983.

What would Tito do if a man with a gun saw him cutting firewood on someone else's land?

"Run away as fast as I can," he answers. "But I always watch out before I start cutting. I'm afraid of the *hacenderos* [the land-owners]."

My romantic notions of rural simplicity are making it difficult for me to comprehend the harshness of life in Tito's village. I keep thinking the place is picturesque. But no, I would not like to live in a leaky thatched-roof hut, without windows, and with rats. Yet the illusion of tropical simplicity remains. The main "street" of Acaya is fringed with flowering trees. Bright salmon-pink clashes with turquoise blue, so much that my eyes miss at first the garbage and the ruts in the road, the stagnant water, and the rusting remains of a truck. The village boasts a church with a bell tower and a store; there is no electric light, no water, no bus service, no school, no telephone. Whenever the kids go to school, which is not often, they have to walk four kilometres to the next village. The women cook on open wood-fires.

Tito doesn't know anybody who has a truck or car, except the police, the *hacendero*, and the priest who comes every second Sunday. A literacy teacher comes on foot once a week. He brings his own lantern and chalkboard. Tito's mother goes to the classes "sometimes" when she is not busy with the kids. She has nine other children besides Tito. His father is usually away either working for a banana company or cutting cane, depend-

Tito.

ing on what work is available.

The banana lands to the north extend further than I can see. Each plant stands eight feet tall, a fierce green row upon row, behind barbed wire. A single line of railroad snakes toward the banana ports, and the train whistle breaks the silence twice a day. Tito's grandfather used to work as a *venenero*, he tells me — the man with the "poison" who sprayed the banana plants. He worked in a gang that lugged the hoses carrying the blue pesticide that dyed their clothes and made them cough up their lungs and become old men at forty.

"My dad says the banana bosses are millionaires. But they don't want any workers now," says Tito. It is true that the "yellow gold" is grown less now in Honduras, as banana companies find other more profitable land in South America. The Honduran land is worn out. Sugar plantations offer back-breaking work for a couple of months a year. Cattle ranches need very few workers. So most of the peasants in Acaya have very little work and very little income. They make less than $10 a week, on a year-round average.

Tito tells me his mother keeps "a few *lempiras*" [worth roughly fifty cents] for some medicine or if somebody has to go to the nearest town, Progreso, in an emergency.

One of his sisters is blind. She was bitten by a *bicho*, an insect. When people are sick, they usually call in the *curandera*, the local healer. She doesn't cost much and she is someone they know and trust. Tito has never been vaccinated against childhood diseases and has never visited a doctor. He's never been to school either.

He refuses to take me inside his little house. I call out, but the voices from inside hush quickly and nobody comes to the open doorway, so I do not intrude.

Later I talk about Tito to a nun who works for a church rural training and development program, not far away. She has lived there for five years and now identifies completely with her peasant community.

"They live like they did two hundred years ago, and they seem so apathetic, right?" she challenges me. "So would you if you suffered from parasites and malnutrition. In the countryside, three out of four people live in extreme poverty. There isn't enough money for food, let alone school books or shoes. This is why the children don't go to school; it is a vicious circle. Without education, they can't climb out of poverty, and without money, they can't get an education.

"When the men try to organize to defend themselves, they are called Communists and cut down by the landowners or the police. I have seen twenty different political murders in this area in the last twelve months. The graves you saw at El Balsamo are those of four ordinary peasants, who went to help fellow workers on strike at a banana plantation. They had a truck and were driving home when two members of the territorial forces stopped them for a ride. The soldiers shot four of them; the other three ran away. They piled the four bodies into the truck and drove off. Other peasants saw the bodies when the truck passed through a village. They stopped it, and the soldiers ran off. They were never prosecuted, though everybody knows who they are."

She did not want me to use her name. "This quietness you see everywhere isn't peace," she says. "It is fear and despair. The children may talk to you because they are not yet aware of the reality."

But even the children in Tito's village are quiet. A very small boy battles a large pig on the end of a string; the pig oinks and scrabbles on the gritty road. The other kids just watch. Most of the day they fetch and carry and look after the little ones, and plant seeds in the bare ground with a digging stick. When the chores are done, they sit listlessly in the dirt.

What sort of games do you play? I ask Tito. But I don't get any answer. Maybe the words are wrong. What do you do when you are not busy doing chores? "I go to sleep," he replies.

The International Labour Organization in Geneva estimates that more than a third of the world's children work, most of them as unpaid family workers. Tito's chores would not even class him as a worker. He is lucky not to be making bricks in forty-degree heat, or working in a carpet factory, or pulling a cart. He has a home, a mother and a father, brothers and sisters. He is not sick or in jail or a victim of war.

Tito is just a typical child of Third World poverty. Nothing special. No emergency. A common case.

Gamero

Everybody calls him by his last name, Gamero, so I do too. Luis Fernando Gamero Escoto, aged thirteen, is a "gentleman student" in the Military School of the North in Honduras. The school is located in a suburb of San Pedro Sula, the country's major industrial town. Colonel Francisco Ruíz Andrade has promised me he would produce three or four typical students, and Gamero is the most talkative.

When I suggest a photograph, he springs to attention so rigidly I expect his shirt buttons to pop. His beret is at just the right angle, his eyes exactly straight ahead, his belt buckle dead centre.

In many ways, Gamero is the sort of teenager a worried mother would love. He is disciplined, incredibly polite, an achiever, athletic, and ambitious. Yet he frightens me.

The school itself looks, as it should, like an expensive private school. It costs $150 for the uniform alone, and $450 for tuition, not including the cost of boarding in the city, for it is a day school. Many Hondurans earn no more than that in a year. When I arrived, some seven hundred students overflowed the parade field, some of them doing push-ups, others deep knee-bends, waiting for the call to attention and announcement of exam results. They politely ignored me as I skirted the field.

In the office of the school psychologist (a motherly woman in army uniform), Gamero and two fellow students are standing "at ease" as if their feet have been measured exactly apart. Gamero relates how he came to go to military school:

"I never did well at regular school. I was never popular and I had no friends. The other boys were always fooling around. They had no ambition and no discipline. They were degenerates.

"I applied to come here when I was eleven, but I didn't make it and I had to wait another year. So I gave up a whole grade to come here, I wanted it so badly. The other students at home told me I was mad."

Gamero broke off all connections with his previous companions and never sees them now, though he comes from San Pedro Sula and lives at home, not far from the school. I question him about his use of the word "degenerate."

"I mean that they smoked and they didn't respect our country. They did not go to church. They laughed at our president. They had no pride in themselves. They were not men — *hombres*. I did not want to be like that.

"I wanted to be somebody. I wanted to have personal security, but I wanted to be part of that security. This school gives me that."

Gamero has to be in class at six-forty-five a.m. and leaves at three p.m. loaded with lots of homework. He takes ordinary academic subjects until eleven a.m. and then has lessons on military tactics, military geography, arms training, military history, strategy, and so on. On weekends, he marches twenty-five kilometres and, when he is a little older, there will be week-long manoeuvres.

As he is only thirteen, he has not yet learned how to use a

gun, but will do so within another year, he expects. He thinks that will be exciting, but a responsibility too. How does he feel about being ordered to kill somebody, or about giving those orders, since he will leave school as a junior officer? Gamero responds in slogans.

"We must defend our country. The enemy wants to destroy our country. We must fight to preserve our traditional values."

"But who is the enemy?" I ask.

"Whoever wants to destroy my country. I am ready to defend my country with my life against those who wish to destroy Honduras."

"But who wants to destroy Honduras?"

Gamero looks momentarily nonplussed, and replies, darkly, "There are always enemies who wish to destroy a country." He refuses to be drawn further, and I sense he is being careful rather than naive.

I ask him if he is Catholic, and he says he is, so I ask how he reconciles killing with the commandment, "Thou shalt not kill." He thinks for almost a whole minute, and then replies smartly as if he has solved a puzzle:

"Our hero Francisco Morazán had to kill to defend his country. It was necessary. I would be like him, and nobody would criticize me for destroying my country's enemies."

Gamero has two ambitions. Either he will leave the army and become a medical doctor, or else he will apply to the Naval College in Chile. Astounded, I ask him what he knows about Chile.

"They have the most famous academy in the world. We all know that. And I want to be the best there is."

I ask him if he knows anything about the history of Chile, about the coup that substituted dictatorship for an elected democracy and led to torture and terror. Gamero says he knows nothing about it and that he is not interested in politics. He pronounces "politics" as if it is a dirty word.

What does he like best about the Military School? "Comradeship. The students here are all friends. We learn not to tease the little ones. We help each other. We respect each other. We respect the traditional values." What are those? "Loyalty to my country, to the Church, and to our traditions."

Gamero's heroes are all Honduran and very respectable. They range from Lempira, the Indian who rebelled against the Spanish conquerors, to Father José Reyes, who founded the university and was Honduras's first poet.

Religion and the army feature as a curious duo in the school's credo. When I meet him, the director tells me he considers the school "a work of God" and the army "the protector of our religion." He says the students participate in masses in honour of fallen soldiers. They also watch movies that show the Honduran army on joint manoeuvres with U.S. forces, designed to repel "Communist" invasion from Nicaragua or Cuba.

"Communism is against God and against our country," Gamero comments, but he does not want to expand.

The Military School of the North is only in its second year, but is planning ahead for warfare that might include nuclear weapons. "Nuclear technology tends to be expanded to other countries, so we have to establish an education that will provide leaders who understand its concepts," explains the director.

And how do Hondurans feel about the school and its students?

"They have won everybody's respect," he replies, pointing out civic projects such as the school's help in a recent vaccination campaign, as well as marches and ceremonies. A poll of parents also gave the school full marks, especially for conduct. Almost all of them indicated they thought the school had "awoken authentic love of country" in their sons.

There are other military academies in Honduras, notably the cadet school in Tegucigalpa, where beplumed, golden-frogged cadets parade like toy soldiers. These students are in great demand for civil events. Gamero's school puts more emphasis on science, technology, and general education and less on tradition. Many students will not make the army their career, they will leave to study for jobs in civil life. But, as Gamero puts it, they "will always be the best."

Jorge

Jorge Alfonso Godoy, aged twenty, is a criminal, a drug addict, and a fount of information on Honduran low-life. We meet at Project Victoria, an hour's drive from Tegucigalpa along the old road to San Pedro Sula. It is Honduras's only treatment centre for young drug addicts and alcoholics, and is funded entirely by local and international private donations.

Jorge has chopped the sleeves off his black T-shirt. Very muscular, with short bushy hair and narrowed eyes, he looks tough. But he is surprisingly polite, even gallant, as he makes sure I get the clean end of the bench. Now that he is going straight and has turned to Christianity, he is as avid to talk about it as any new member of Alcoholics Anonymous, except that he really used to have a good time smoking marijuana. What a shame it is all over!

Nobody I can find has any figures on drug addiction or crime in Honduras, only the acknowledgement that both are on the increase. Shoeshine boys smoke pot or sniff glue down by the river. Slum-dwellers make their own *guaro* or hooch. Cocaine is starting to come in, for the pleasure of the few rich. All drug-users are either criminals or close to criminal activity, because that is the only way to afford drugs. This is Jorge's story:

"I began smoking pot when I was thirteen and my father died. I failed first year of high school. My mother was mad with me. I wanted to leave home, but didn't have any money, so I stole $1,500 from her. Where did it all go? Who knows? Anyway, I spent it all on parties. I didn't dare go home because I felt so ashamed. I had no idea what to do.

"Then I found I didn't have to decide what to do because the army picked me up and I had to do two years' military service."

I checked Jorge's age at the time, anxious to know if there really were kids that young in the army.

"I was still thirteen when they grabbed me for the army. A lot of kids were that young. Nowadays they are supposed to be more careful who they pick up, but back in 1977 nobody cared as long as you were taller than the gun, and I was a big kid. It wasn't such a bad life. We had cocaine, peyote, and we made *pochanga* [alcohol and cola].

"I lived alone when I got out. I've always been a loner. I tried to go back to school and give up smoking pot, but couldn't do it. I robbed my mother again. She said she never wanted to see me again and sent for the police. So I left the country and went to Guatemala. They jailed me for three months and then deported me, but my mother would not have me in the house.

"So I found an old school friend who was now a professional

Jorge Alfonso Godoy.

thief and we went into business. We robbed houses and cars. The very first day, we stole $8,000. We rented a house and a car and we had everything. I had a girlfriend living with me, a new suit, guns, papers, a bank account, and I was only sixteen. We began to get in deeper.

"I met a Nicaraguan who sold marijuana by the pound and was in the gun trade. He said he had killed several guys, and I believed him. Once, when we went to collect from some customers, I shot a *campesino* and I was terrified I had killed him. I went back to make sure he was just winged in the arm. I was scared of going to hell, not just of the police.

"We used to hold up the rich people coming out of the Maya Hotel casino. We had credit cards. We sold currency and gold. I suppose we weren't as good at it as we thought we were, because the police surrounded us one evening, sixteen of them. They beat us up badly. They claimed we were guerrillas and photographed us with Salvadorean FMLN propaganda. But that was a lie. I'd never have anything to do with guerrillas because that's even more dangerous than crime. They held me thirty-seven days incommunicado, handcuffed behind my back and blindfolded. They were really rough. They threatened to kill us. They thought we must be guerrillas, because we had $16,000 on us, and we had guns and radio equipment we had stolen. But that was all for us.

"Well, in Honduras, you can get out of anything so long as you have money and friends. My mother knew a police captain; somebody paid somebody else off, and I was a free man. That's how things work.

"My mother took me back in and I tried to go straight. But when I looked for work, they would see my record and refuse to hire me. I started stealing again, just small stuff, picking pockets. I was inside for three months on a gun charge. Then my friends wanted me to go to New York. I knew that would be the big time, and I didn't really want to end up my life getting killed so far from home. And for what? For a few hours feeling good on pot or liquor?

"I was twenty, and I had ruined my life already. I had smoked pot for seven years. About seventy per cent of the kids I knew smoked. I smoked fifteen to twenty joints a day, at $2.50 a joint, so I had to steal to pay for it. I did morning glory too. That stuff put me in hospital twice, with overdoses. But I felt fine; no medical effects. Except, of course, that I was sick with worry about getting caught when I was stealing, so it wasn't that much fun. I knew I had to make a decision to stop but I didn't think I was strong enough to do it.

"Somebody told me about Project Victoria. All you had to do was walk up to the office of the Brigade of Christian Love and fill in the forms. Waiting those nineteen days before they accepted me was the hardest time of my life. I just stayed in bed. Did I smoke? Sure, but my mother never knew. She is so easy to take in. But I prayed, lots. I never used to have any use for religion, but I needed help. God was the only person around I could talk to. My old friends would have laughed at me."

Jorge moved in to Project Victoria expecting to stay at the farm at least six months, maybe a year. At Christmas time he would be offered a pass to go home, but he decided to wait until January. The Christmas celebrations would be just too much temptation, he explains.

The patients at Project Victoria range in age from fourteen to thirty. Some can contribute towards the cost of the treatment: a blend of group therapy, Christianity, hard work, and athletics. They have a full-time doctor and psychologist, facilities for soccer, basketball, and weights, and a library. They even have a couple of horses that belong to the staff but are available to anyone who has to make a quick trip to town, six kilometres away. Jorge is on kitchen duty, which he doesn't like but knows he has to do. He is anxious to get on to carpentry, hoping to learn sufficient skill to find a job when he leaves. All the boys help on the farm. Several boys are brushing and petting a real Jersey cow and her calf while I talk to Jorge.

Why is there such a drug problem in Honduras? I ask him.

"I suppose it's part of progress. Drugs are available, so the kids get them and steal to get more. It's the thing to do. The old folk get drunk. The little kids are on glue at as young as ten years old. I feel sorry for them because they're really screwed up. It curdles your brain. But they don't care because it makes them feel good at the time.

"Then the kids see these stars on TV and know they are on cocaine. So, what the hell? Why not?

"There is a lot of influence from the United States. The kids think that anything from the United States is bound to be good. A lot of kids travel to the States. They hitchhike, get deported, get worked to death, or get taken for a ride by the coyotes who take their money to smuggle them across the border. They think it is a great adventure, and then they find themselves sitting on the floor in some jail.

"But there's nothing much to look forward to for a kid. No jobs. Schools are a joke. There aren't any places you can work out or play soccer. It's a bad business, being young. And once you are on drugs, and stealing to get them, nobody is going to help you stop.

"If I hadn't listened to God speaking to me, I'd be out there now, holding you up outside your hotel."

Jorge isn't even allowed to smoke a cigarette in Project Victoria, but he eats well and has put on weight and muscle. He knows the project's success rate isn't any miracle, only thirty-three per cent, but it is the only treatment centre, and without it none of the boys are likely to make it on their own.

Felipe

Felipe is thin, brave, and nervous. Aged twenty, he has a job that pays nothing at all and isn't listed in any category on employment forms: he is a slum organizer. He met me in secret and was justifiably concerned about whether his photograph would appear, because slum organizing does not make one popular with the Honduran police.

It is hard to find out much personal information, because Felipe always speaks of "we," not "me." He grew up in a village called El Paraíso [Paradise] that was anything but idyllic. His family was very poor and there were five children. They moved to Tegucigalpa in 1979 to find work. Felipe started working when he was twelve, at odd jobs and in the harvest. He passed Grade Six, but found no steady work. What he did find was that thousands of Hondurans were like him. Now he lives and works in one of the *barrios* of Tegucigalpa.

"The city is divided into what we call *patronatos* or districts," he explains. "Half a million people live in Tegucigalpa. Eighty per cent of them are poor, unorganized, and unrepresented. You can see the old tiled roofs and twisting, cobbled streets that lead to dirt tracks where the old silver mines used to be. It sounds fascinating in the tourist literature. Believe me, it is no fun at all to live there. The Americans and the rich, secluded in their new homes, never know how the rest of the people of Tegucigalpa live.

"Then there is Comayagüela, on the other side of the river, where the tourists never go. It is dirty, ugly, and miserable. There are no parks, no trees, no neighbourhood centres; just slums."

Felipe is involved in helping slum-dwellers organize and demand their rights to housing and city services. The *patronatos*, he explains, used to be governed by politicians who didn't even live in the *barrio*; maybe they had a store there, but they never represented the people in the slums. Now, the *patronato* committees are using legal means to get their rights.

"Honduran people have been too patient, too humble, for too long, but they are waking up and taking charge now." Felipe offers me examples of what he means by this.

In his *patronato*, seventy per cent of the people who live there are unemployed. So the men got together to form workshops, where they make pots and pans and shoes. They had the skills from their previous jobs, and they scrounged for materials at first. They found they could sell for less than factory prices. Moreover, the experience taught them that the factories had exploited their labour and cheated the customers.

Getting enough food to eat is as big a problem as finding a job. Two or three dollars a day won't buy enough food for a family, not even the beans and tortillas that constitute the staple diet of Hondurans. Very few people eat eggs, meat, fruit, or vegetables. The most popular Christmas treat is an imported apple, but it costs fifty cents. Oranges grow in the countryside, but they are green and not much eaten. They're not exported and rarely reach city markets. Health workers are trying to promote them as a good source of vitamins, but merchants would rather make a bigger profit on imported apples.

Housing is another headache. The slums of Tegucigalpa have no electricity, no sewage system, not even standpipes for water let alone running water in each house. The water man charges $3 for a barrel of water. Houses are built from waste cardboard.

"We don't just want building materials. We are demanding wages for those who build their houses," says Felipe. "These people have a right to housing and to self-respect. Their hands are not free; they shouldn't work for nothing on city projects that the government ought to provide."

According to Tegucigalpa municipal authorities, eighty per cent of those living in the slums have come from the country looking for work, but very few ever find jobs, and most are illiterate.

"That's why we have to provide an education in how to fight for their rights, how to live in a city, how to help each other."

Felipe works on a radio program, the Voice of the Community, that is broadcast every Sunday morning. It teaches public health, voices complaints, and gives people a chance to talk about their needs and ambitions. Right now, the program is promoting a campaign to improve the street system — if you can call dirt roads that are caved in or slick with mud-slides a street system. Every week, more *campesinos* arrive in the city. It takes three years on average for the city to approve sales of land lying vacant so that the newcomers can build their own homes. Felipe takes me to visit "an invasion," a common Latin-American term for a land take-over. Two thousand families applied in 1981 for some city land and saved $250,000 to pay for city services, not expecting something for nothing. They had been assured it was city property, and that it would be only a matter of time before they would be able to take possession. They waited three years and decided they were not going to wait any longer.

The land they have occupied is bare rock, with a few scrubby bushes flattened by the wind. We scramble up to find the slum-dwellers' representative face to face with the police. Apparently an army captain has suddenly claimed that all this land belongs to her.

The people are not going to give in. They have fixed the Honduran flag to the top of a tent, where it flaps noisily in the stiff wind. Women working in a kitchen under the cover of a plastic shelter are already feeding the population. But I can't figure out where they sleep. All I can see are piles of grass and branches apparently ready for burning. To my surprise I'm told the piles have been heaped up to shelter poorly-clad women and children from the raw winds that scour the hills. This is where they live. Once, the hills yielded the silver that made Tegucigalpa rich. Now they are known as the "hills of misery."

"In the hills, the poor are even closer to heaven," says the newspaper headline reporting this invasion.

"It is this kind of thinking that makes it so hard for Hondurans to stand up and fight for their rights," comments Felipe. "If editors think it is heaven to sleep under a pile of leaves and be threatened by the police, that shows how divorced from reality the newspapers and most rich Hondurans are."

Felipe's own parents are apolitical. At first they were horrified by their son's political activities and very much afraid of the authorities. They did not want to lose what little they had by claiming rights to more, but Felipe encouraged them to take part in an invasion.

"Now they live on what we call 'recuperated' land. They have a decent house, and there is a communal water supply, with a tap at the end of the road. It is not ideal, but it is better. And they feel good because they fought for it. They understand me now. They didn't, before."

The young men and women thronging Tegucigalpa's doughnut shops, especially "Dunkin Donuts" (all the names are English), wouldn't understand either. They wear school uniforms, flock to movies like "Conan the Destroyer," and worship Michael Jackson. When I asked them about their ambitions, "getting out of Honduras" or "going to America" were the most common replies.

I ask Felipe if he feels lonely as an activist, working clandestinely amid a general climate of apathy and indifference.

"But I am not alone," he tries to explain. "You think of all young people as being alike. Here, poor and rich teenagers are as different as that old man begging, and the old man who owns a bank.

"I haven't been to a movie in three years. I've got less than a dollar in my pockets, look. But somebody will feed me tonight. I can find a place to sleep in dozens of houses where the people know me and share what little they have. They are my people, not the kids who go to private schools."

What about any plans to get married, have children, to have what we would call a "normal" life?

"Too much to do," he replies.

Felipe's eyes are burning, his skin is pale, and his shoulders stand out sharply under his thin shirt. He stirs all my motherly feelings, but I feel helpless to do anything. I buy him some hot soup and give him a bag of apples. I have a feeling he won't save even one apple for himself.

Edith

Edith's dad didn't want her training with the boys. He kept on yelling at her, and wanted her home where he could keep an eye on her. Finally, he threw her out.

It isn't easy to be an athlete in Honduras, especially for a woman. At age sixteen Edith Ramírez is one of her country's most promising runners, but she gets little help from either her family or country.

I meet her at the volleyball courts, where she is doing stretching exercises along with a dozen or so boys. The only place she can run is at the soccer stadium and, even then, she runs only once a week. There isn't a single athletic track in the whole of Honduras.

Edith's best distance is 1,500 metres, but she usually runs in marathons of up to twenty kilometres because they give her a chance to compete with other runners. That means male competition, because there are so few women athletes in Honduras. In her first year of running, Edith came third in Central American events in San Salvador and Costa Rica, but, as she has no women competitors in her own country, she runs with the boys.

"That's the problem," she sighs. She is a leggy and very attractive teenager, and she shyly admits that the boys call her "the flying kiss."

"That's the boys at school. They always talk like that. But the boys I train with take me seriously because I can outrun a lot of them. Since I've been a teenager I've always had a problem being taken seriously. Before that, I played soccer with the boys and ran races. We were all barefoot, and I was accepted as one of them. Then they started to whistle at me and act silly, and my girlfriends could think about nothing but boys.

"I like boys, but they can't seem to separate my being a girl from my being a runner. That's why I hate that nickname. The boys I run with aren't like that."

But Edith's dad couldn't see the difference. Edith was out after school with a lot of boys, and it made no difference to him if she was running or if she was fooling around with them. Worse still, she went off for track meets to other countries with a lot of boys. He threatened to throw her out of the house several times. Finally, he did so. Her mother was no help, as she was utterly cowed by her husband. So Edith went to live with friends of her athletics coach. This was the only way she could get the food an athlete needs.

"Edith comes from a poor family. When we discovered her she was running barefoot in street races in a poor *barrio*. She doesn't get fruit, she doesn't get eggs, she doesn't get milk, unless we provide them for her. You can't be an athlete if you suffer from malnutrition," her coach explains.

"The only sport that gets government support in Honduras is soccer. Everything else has to limp along as best as it can."

When she lived at home, Edith had to share a bedroom with her two brothers. They definitely got preferential treatment, especially from her dad. Now she is in Grade Six and is a reasonable student, I am told. She wants to become a doctor, but doesn't have much confidence in realizing her ambitions, because of lack of money and because she's a woman.

"I'm basically a happy person. I don't worry. Even if my dad throws me out, somebody will give me a bed."

She feels happiest of all when she is running; it is a way of forgetting about problems, and a way of competing and winning respect. "I'm sure my dad thinks I will end up a prostitute, on the street, because I get along easily with boys. But I know I won't. They respect me."

Edith considers herself "very sentimental." When I asked her what had been her saddest moment, she tells me it was when her grandfather died.

"I never really knew him and that makes me sad — that people can die and you never got close to them. I want to have a very close family when I get married." But she is in no hurry to do so. She doesn't want to be limited. She thinks girls who get married before they are twenty, as most Honduran women do, are "stupid" because they will never have any freedom.

Edith says she has no interest in politics, no opinions about the government, about the United States, or about Central American conflicts. But she is angry about the lack of support for sports. She does have a sense that she is "different" from her mother and most Honduran women. She knows that there are other young women like her, but no one calls her a feminist, the word is foreign.

"We are a surprise to our families. There is no way we will be stuck at home, hidden from society, like other generations of females," she tells me. But she knows of no national women's organizations. Neither do I, not even after six weeks of looking for groups whose exclusive concern is women's rights.

Only one organization, the Honduran Federation of Peasant Women (FEHMUC), represents women's demands. About five thousand women are organized in some three hundred local groups, in order "to be a powerful agent for social change and play a vital role in creating, promoting and protecting our own socio-economic development," as their pamphlets state. They have come a long way from their origins as "housewives' clubs" organized by the Catholic Church. If the FEHMUC statement of principles and objectives sounds a mite optimistic, the FEHMUC women are certainly not naive. When I speak to Julia Saldana, one of the leaders, she talks less about an abstract need for social change than about training classes, health clinics, and loans for women's co-operatives.

"We are not working from our anger at being forced into a secondary role. We are working from women's strengths," she explains. "For example, there is a tremendous shortage of medicine in Honduras and people cannot afford it even if they can actually find it. Instead of looking for doctors and pills, we remembered that women had managed pretty well before the pills arrived. So we sent for an expert in natural health, who taught many women how to use local plants to make infusions, poultices, and cures for diarrhoea. Women can afford them and all they have to do is relearn what their grandmothers knew. Then we can do without medical technology.

"We are working on soya milk and other foods we never knew about, too. We are very practical in our efforts, but as women learn to take charge of their own health and nutrition, they grow in strength as people, too."

Earlier, I had visited a typical FEHMUC project on the Atlantic coast, where forty-seven women prepare snack foods made from yuca plants. Yuca is a staple food of black women on the coast. Now they are growing and cooking it, and packaging it into "munchies" for movie-goers in the city. For the first time they can now support their families when their menfolk are working on the banana boats.

Among the women in the project there was a lot of good-natured raillery about the laziness of men. It is a part of the warm, mutual support that all the women, from age sixteen to seventy, have developed. I am reminded of this community while Edith talks of her own isolation. I ask her if she gets support from the other girls at school. Do they understand her prob-

Edith Ramírez.

lems at home and her ambitions in the athletic world?

"Not very much," she replies. "I have friends, of course, but most of the girls at school are competing for boyfriends, going through that stage when another girl is a rival. There is mutual complaining about parents who won't let girls go out, but I can't say we support each other much.

"That's something that has to come in the future."

Eduardo's Class

The kids in Eduardo Bähr's class are part of an "experiment." They make up plays and stories, paint whatever they want, yell in class, and fall about in hysterical giggles. Such a class would be routine for one of the more creative and permissive North American or British schools, but in Honduras, where rote learning and straight lines dominate teaching techniques, this class is exceptional.

It is possible because the Higher Education Institute that trains teachers needs such "experimental" classes to practise on. It is hoped that the student teachers will eventually pass on what they've learned to other kids. But it will take years for such non-authoritarian concepts of learning to offset the rigidity and mean-spiritedness of the Honduran education system.

For me, the kids in Bähr's class are a reminder that imagination cannot be taught; it is a natural plant that either dies or flourishes, according to its nurture.

The Grade Three kids have made up their own stories and are taping them for a radio program. The one that the kids voted the best is about a little stream. The stream runs through the poor part of town, where there are stones, tin cans, and rats, and it runs through the garden of the president, where there are flowers and fruit trees, and then it runs down to the sea, where it joins with all the other streams. All the drops of water are equal in the big sea.

The Grade Four kids have painted pictures. Their paintings show mothers breast-feeding their babies, tall office buildings, streets with lights and cars and fire trucks. In many other schools copying is still the only way art is taught, but these children are allowed to paint whatever they want. Surprisingly, none of them try to depict what they have seen on TV.

The drama class is the most fun of all. The kids have collaborated to put on the story of the Pied Piper of Hamelin, with a few contemporary touches. The boys have made their own rat costumes. The shoemaker, the people's leader in the story, is played by a girl. The town mayor and councillors are shown as buffoons and hypocrites. But the kids obviously like the arguments between the people and the rich folk best of all.

In their version, the city officials will not help the people get rid of the rats until their own factories, and the mayor's house, are invaded by the rats. They arrest the shoemaker when he protests. The rat-catcher refuses to go after the rats until the shoemaker is freed and the mayor apologizes to the people and promises financial aid.

The kids know what it was all about because they come from a poor *barrio* nearby. They are in their element when they scream at the authorities and free the shoemaker from jail.

"Of course, it is all about history, about Hamelin, remember. Nobody could accuse us of encouraging children to protest against authority. It is a story, yes," a teacher advises me.

I understand. A couple of years earlier, when students at the national university put on a drama that necessitated the use of prop guns, right-wing newspapers splashed headlines about guerrilla training on the campus across their front pages.

The children in the experimental classes are going to make their own scenery, record their own music, and present the play to other classes. In doing so, they learn how to combine art forms and how to organize the work themselves. It is a remarkable endeavour in the desert of Honduran cultural aridity. Not only is there no government money for culture, either adult- or child-oriented: there is no encouragement at all.

In Honduras I watched a children's TV show, absolutely the worst I have ever seen. In between candy commercials, child after child imitated Michael Jackson or else silently mouthed American pop songs emanating from a scratchy record player. This appeared to be typical programming for children's TV.

The National Ballet presented a gala program in Tegucigalpa while I was there. All the pieces were classical ballet, performed bravely but not very well. Anyhow, since there were only thirty-five of us in the audience, despite the fact that the performance was free, what did it matter? The students had to finance it themselves.

Children's books available in Honduras are almost entirely Spanish versions of supermarket Disney, with pictures of Western kids munching hamburgers and skate-boarding down California boulevards. In Tegucigalpa's two main bookstores there are no Latin American authors and no Latin American settings. Even the Disney books are too expensive for most families. Comic books, sold in the markets, are hardly for kids; most are about space wars or real wars, and a number are blatantly pornographic.

I didn't know that Eduardo Bähr, from the experimental class, wrote children's books until I discovered an eight-page colouring book by him in Tegucigalpa's progressive bookstore. It was called *Mazapán* and it was the only children's book I found where the kids looked Central American. In the book the children have a tortoise called "bureaucracy," a dog that pees on plants, and a parrot that bites, and they visit a park that has a model of the Mayan city of Copán.

The ruins of Copán themselves have been totally neglected, there is so little national pride in Honduras. There is no road to them from the capital city; even the national airline has no regular flights. Tourists wanting to see Honduras's archeological treasures are advised to do so from Guatemala.

No guide book to Honduras existed until a modest little book called *Get To Know Honduras* came out in 1984. It is no more than a dreary collection of statistics about the number of telephones and the consumption of water, with a few facts on mountains and parks. It does not mention a single Honduran hero, artist, writer, thinker, teacher, musician, or sportsplayer. The only "artists" mentioned are the composers of the national anthem. With such little information about themselves, who is there for a Honduran kid to emulate?

A Canadian who has lived in Honduras for three years told me how unhappy she was to find so much apathy there. Even the kids, she said, have so little life, so little curiosity, so little creativity. But the kids playing rats and rebellious citizens in Eduardo's class hadn't lacked life or enthusiasm. Just a little encouragement had made them flower.

Later, at a refugee agency, I saw pictures by Salvadorean refugee kids in Honduran camps. They were remarkable, not just because of the horrors they depicted — grinning men with guns, dismembered bodies — but because of their artistic quality. Art, or any form of self-expression, is not only of great value in helping kids to bring their terrors out into the open and to order their experiences; but it can also be used, if it is exhibited widely enough, to draw attention to the plight of the refugees.

Angelita (left) from El Salvador, and Rosario of Nicaragua, play together in a co-operative camp in Nicaragua.

The faces of the new Nicaragua — three dancers at the Granada children's festival.

■
Part Four

NICARAGUA

THE BEST WAY to appreciate what Nicaragua has accomplished since the revolution in 1979 is to fly there direct from Honduras. Once Nicaragua was in much the same shape as Honduras, but today it is hard to make comparisons. In one hour I flew from begging children and despair to the sight of children planting flowers: children who have faith in the future.

It took me a day or two to adjust to being in Managua, or even to find Managua at all among the earth-shaken gaps that had once been the centre of a modern city. Picking my way across downtown fields, I got lost following directions that referred to long-gone landmarks. I got hot and tired waiting for buses or fighting to board them, and frustrated trying to flag disdainful taxi-drivers. I was told they didn't stop for gringos because gringos never knew where they were going (true, alas!), but that didn't reconcile me to trudging miles in forty-degree heat.

Then my frustrations began to melt and Managua began to enchant me. I walked everywhere, even at midnight, alone. The only dangers I encountered were the occasional horse or goat grazing downtown, or gaping holes in the sidewalk. I started to feel quite romantic over the empty spaces. Bushes, purple and yellow with flowers and filled with birds, stud the empty spaces. But then a neighbourhood kid led me off the path to show me why the fields have been left downtown: under the bushes and flowers they've built air-raid shelters, in anticipation of U.S. bombs.

More than any other country I have visited, Nicaragua defies definition. Television broadcasts a baseball game from Yankee Stadium followed by a lesson in operating a rocket launcher. On TV I watched President Daniel Ortega and Fred Flintstone, a Mexican soap opera slippery with tears and a news item showing the bodies of Nicaraguan teenagers burned alive by counter-revolutionaries.

Anticipating military parades, I found all the kids downtown for *Purísima*, the Catholic Festival of the Annunciation. Wooden toys and grapefruit were handed out to thousands of kids, and in every neighbourhood there was a week of ceremonies around the local shrine. I saw housewives lining up, I assumed for food until I realized they were waiting their turn for rifle training.

What I saw could substantiate any of the differing North American opinions of Nicaragua. Yes, I saw beggars, but I saw very few barefoot kids. Yes, I saw lineups for meat, but I found milk, eggs, bread, and fruit everywhere and cheap. I heard experts tell me Nicaragua was halfway to paradise and others who told me it was an economic basket-case. I watched women raging at the U.S. Embassy for its support of counter-revolutionaries who had kidnapped their children, and I listened to furious women denounce the Sandinista government for calling up their sons for military service. I saw tanks in the neighbourhood parks, but I saw them swarmed over by kids who drew all over the sides when the soldiers weren't looking.

As I had just come from the apathetic despair of Honduras, I was bewildered, a little shocked, but delighted by the enthusiasm and vitality of Nicaraguans. Seeing Nicaragua from this perspective made me want to shake every fat matron who bemoaned the toothpaste shortage, every spoiled private-school kid who didn't want to do military service, every foreign journalist who judged Nicaragua by Western standards and blamed the Sandinistas for lack of spare auto-parts.

Most amazing, to me, was the freedom of speech. I had rather looked forward to reading *La Prensa*, touted as the bastion of freedom by liberals of the West. When I read it, instead of the critical analysis I'd expected, I found social notes about birthday babies, señorita or señorito this and that, pictured in ruffles and bows. The rest of the newspaper was divided between sexploitation and nasty cracks or deliberate lies about the government. Why do people buy it? I asked, and was told it reminded the bourgeoisie of the "good old days" of the dictator Somoza. His followers were still around, bemoaning their loss of power, but still making plenty of money as, true to their promise, the Sandinistas allow private as well as public enterprise.

On a bus, a handsome young man, cradling an equally handsome baby, told me, in a loud voice, that he didn't like the Sandinistas. When I asked why, he told me they had jailed him for two years. When I asked what he had done to deserve that sentence he replied without any embarrassment that he had killed a Sandinista. Was this the terror described in U.S. propaganda?

As everybody in Nicaragua speaks his or her mind, it is easy for a visitor to gather a multiplicity of confusing impressions. However, there were four points on which everybody I spoke to agreed:

First, they would never return to the past. Even the paving stones Managuans walk on remind them of the dictator Somoza. Somoza's own factory made them after the 1972 earthquake, and made millions of dollars in the process. In 1976, only sixty-eight per cent of primary-school children actually registered for classes and half of these dropped out before the end of Grade One. Only ten per cent of teenagers attended high school.[12] Illiteracy was eighty per cent in the countryside, and infant mortality there was the highest in Central America (140 per thousand).[13] International aid had changed nothing. When Somoza fled with his $200 million private fortune, he left behind fifty thousand dead, two hundred thousand homeless, forty thousand orphans, and a total of debt, capital flight, and war destruction that exceeded $4 billion.

Second, they would never welcome a U.S. invasion. National pride had flowered in the wake of the counter-revolutionary atrocities, U.S. threats, the mining of ports, and the sight of spy planes overhead. *No pasarán* — they shall not pass — was everybody's slogan. It was a reaction based on years of U.S. intervention in Central America. The phrase most often repeated to me

[12] George Black, *Loss of Fear: Education in Nicaragua Before and After the Revolution* (London: World University Service, 1980).

[13] Peter Rosset and John Vandermeer, eds., *The Nicaraguan Reader: Documents of a Revolution Under Fire* (New York: Grove, 1983).

was a remark made by Franklin Roosevelt about Somoza in 1948: "He's a sonofabitch, but he's ours."

Third, they hated the counter-revolutionaries. They might be "freedom fighters" to Ronald Reagan, but they were mercenaries and monsters to Nicaraguans, even to those who detested the Sandinistas, even to the man on the bus who had himself killed a Sandinista.

Fourth, they were afraid. After the invasion of Grenada, they had waited for an attack by the U.S. or Honduras. They had turned on their radios with trepidation, waiting for the other shoe to drop, as one woman put it to me. They were past trying to understand U.S. motives, or the U.S. preoccupation with Nicaraguan politics.

"We're a dinky little country, the same size as England and Wales. We are dirt poor. We have so few aircraft it was hard to assemble helicopters to transport the Pope and his retinue. It makes no sense at all to picture us as Communist aggressors about to attack Washington," said an English-speaking businessman who had spent half his life in New York and who said he still didn't understand the Americans.

Whether they understand U.S. motives or not, Nicaraguans still live under the shadow of U.S. aircraft. The bombs could come any time, and it would be easy to destroy Managua, to complete the work of the earthquake. But the Nicaraguans will never give in. An old man sitting in the park told me his favourite grandson was a militia leader.

"I never did much because I didn't know how to change things. But Carlos, he's different. He's only seventeen but he knows so much. He's a radio mechanic. He can make speeches. He has a gun that can shoot down aircraft. He knows what he is fighting for."

Like many others, the old man thought it would be a long war if the Yankees did invade. Men like Carlos would hole up in the hills, for years if necessary, but in the end they would come down again and bring the revolution back with them.

It sounded a grim future for the children of Nicaragua, but the faces in my camera lens were radiant: militia girls with dangling earrings, soldiers off duty reading cartoons and flirting, kids with open, happy faces. When the heat drops after school, after work, Managuans congregate downtown in a little park named after a kid called "Cricket" — Luis Alfonso Velásquez. He was a student revolutionary who used to beg for money and make bombs and barricades. The National Guard killed him in the year of the revolution, 1979. He was only nine years old.

Ana, 19, despite the earrings a much respected militia officer in the coffee area.

Brenda

Brencha Rocha literally gave her right arm for the Nicaraguan Revolution in 1982, when she was fifteen. I don't know what to say to her. That empty right sleeve drags my eyes from her shy smile, chubby face, and mop of unruly hair as we sit talking in the little house that is headquarters in Managua for the Association of Sandinista Children (ANS).

The children of Nicaragua trouble me profoundly. They are brave, gentle, beautiful, fierce in their patriotism, and they are dying every day. Six thousand children have been orphaned by the contra attacks from the Honduran border; 134 children under the age of twelve have been killed since 1981, plus another 3,213 teenagers. While I was there, each week more teenagers went into the danger zone to pick coffee. Twenty-four thousand of them have enrolled in the "production brigades." Other teenagers protect them, carrying seven-pound anti-aircraft M-44s as easily as North American kids carry their backpacks to summer camp.

Nicaragua is a country of children — forty-two per cent of the population is under sixteen. Teenagers insisted on voting in the 1984 elections, so the voting age was lowered to sixteen. The officials I meet in government offices are in their early twenties, and the people who organize health and defence and social programs even younger. The literacy campaign teachers who turned the country round from eighty per cent illiteracy to eighty per cent literacy were as young as twelve, and a number of them were killed during that campaign. The Association of Sandinista children is named after the FSLN's youngest hero, nine-year-old Luis Alfonso Velásquez.

How am I going to bridge the gap between North American children — the "Me" generation — and these kids? The Nicaraguans make me ashamed, defensive, apologetic for my own children and grandchildren; they embarrass me. They challenge my Western notions about the vulnerability of kids, the need for kids to play and be protected from the real world. Kids in Nicaragua play a crucial role in that real world. They bear enormous burdens of responsibility, both now, and for the future, because any revolution is pregnant with the future generation, the better world.

Brenda Rocha.

I feel that if I can understand Brenda Rocha, maybe I can also understand Nicaraguan children better, feel easier, less heartsick for their sacrifices and their certainties.

Brenda was only thirteen when she joined the Sandinista Youth. At age fifteen, she went with the militia to the north of Nicaragua, to help protect local peasants from attacks by the contras coming down from the Honduran border.

"We were sent there in July 1982. There was a fiesta in the village — the contras always seem to use times like that to attack. A peasant ran into the dance to say a large band of contras was coming. We, that is eight of us kids in the militia, managed to get the children and the old people into some trenches we had dug. But there were about a hundred armed contras, and we weren't very good at fighting. We kept on shooting for hours, but there were too many of them and they over-ran us. All my friends were killed. They shot me twice in the legs and in my right arm. I fell beside the others, but I could still see.

"The contras came up and they began to cut the heads off my friends and I was terrified they would do the same with me.

But one of the contras started shouting that the Nicaraguan army was coming, so they all fled. The army got me to hospital, but it was too late to save my right arm. My legs were not badly damaged, but they had to cut off the arm at the shoulder."

Eventually Brenda got a prosthesis. She spent months learning how to use it, but never became happy with it. Now, it stays in her closet. She manages very well, she insists, with her left hand. She taught herself to write left-handed, how to dress and eat single-handedly, and how to type. She works a full day at the ANS office, organizing children's events, children's radio programs, and the ANS publications, which range from colouring books to histories of the Sandinista movement.

"The ANS wasn't formed *for* children. It was formed *by* children. They had fought in the revolution, kids as young as eight or nine, and they were not going to let anybody keep them out. From that time onwards, the children have been leaders in our society. If something has to be done — a vaccination program against a new infection, an emergency call for help in the harvest — children are the ones who choose to get it done."

The ANS has two age levels. Kids between seven and ten years old are called the *mascots*, and wear blue kerchiefs. The *carlitos*, between ages eleven and fourteen, wear black and red kerchiefs. They were named after Carlos Fonseca. Carlos Fonseca, founder of the Sandinista National Liberation Front (FSLN), was killed by Somoza's guards on November 7, 1976, three years before the Sandinista victory. He had sold newspapers on the streets of Matagalpa from the age of nine until he was fourteen. He continued to go to school even when he was working in the mines, and was always the best student in his year, despite his revolutionary activities: he got a B.A. and a gold medal and went on to study economics. For the ANS, education is children's main duty. While they help in neighbourhood projects like clean-up, or go to the country to pick coffee, schooling still matters most.

I question Brenda about defence, and the stories I have heard of kids trailing rifles bigger than themselves.

"Sure, there were kids with guns in the revolution. They had fought the National Guard with stones, so when there was a chance for them to grab guns from the guards, of course they did so. But don't get the idea we encourage kids to have guns. We don't. That is for sixteen-year-olds and up. And even with them, guns are not a toy or something to be used to threaten others with. You won't hear about hold-ups and murders by teenagers here, only about the murder of kids trying to defend their country."

Brenda is very proud of the inventive work done by kids. In their science projects, they had devised ways to make shoepolish and ways to use waste bananas. The government takes their research seriously, instead of giving them a pat on the head.

"That's the difference, that we take children seriously in Nicaragua. We mature earlier here, too; a girl of sixteen is ready for marriage, and a seventeen-year-old is a man. But we believe that children much younger can and should contribute to their society. If you expect a lot from them, they will give a lot, and grow up to your expectations. If a country marginalizes its children, leaves them to beg in the streets, the kids will grow up useless to their country, and unhappy with themselves. Kids are capable of so much more than we think."

Brenda wants to have kids of her own. She looks very feminine, with tiny earrings and a gentle manner. She loves dancing, and would grow flowers if only there were somewhere to grow them in the backyard of her family home. Maybe, some day, she will get married and have kids and flowers — one day when kids no longer have to fight and get killed.

The next day, I am walking down a dusty street when I see a little girl patting a small yellow flower into the arid dirt under one of the stunted trees of Managua. She has water for it, in a cup.

"What are you planting it for?" I ask, thinking it might be part of an organized school project, or an ANS campaign.

"Because it is beautiful," she whispers.

Deborah

Revolution isn't a magic wand of salvation. In Nicaragua's Atlantic Coast region it created almost as many problems as it solved. So says Deborah Robb, an eighteen-year-old Sandinista militant whose mother is Miskito Indian and her father Caribbean Black. She has come to Managua to learn journalism in a training scheme at the Sandinista newspaper *Barricada*. She will return home to Bluefields when she's finished her training because she wants to help the Atlantic Coast have its own revolution, an authentic one.

"It won't work if it is imported, however much good will there is," she insists. "That is what went wrong. There is a better understanding, now, on the Atlantic Coast, but it would not be honest to tell you things are going fine."

A tall young woman with an Afro haircut, she still feels as if she were in a foreign country in Managua. She says the food is different, there's no coco oil, not much fish or meat and too much rice and tortillas. Most people are Catholic, not Protestant. There is a subtle racial discrimination, so vague she finds it difficult to fight, but still there. Blacks are distrusted because of suspected connections with the contras invading Nicaragua from Honduras. This is a suspicion founded on an age-old colour prejudice that nobody will admit to, but she can feel from the way people stare, or their awkward politeness.

"I don't blame the Sandinistas for that," she says. "It is history. The Atlantic Coast has always been separate from the rest of Nicaragua. The tension began when we met each other for the first time."

The Atlantic Coast comprises fifty-six per cent of Nicaraguan territory, its entire eastern half, but it has only twelve per cent of the population. Spain never colonized the Atlantic. In the seventeenth century, Britain established a Miskito kingdom among the Indian population, using them in battles with the Spanish, and the kingdom lasted until 1860. The Atlantic Coast region was finally incorporated into the rest of Nicaragua in 1894. More English influence arrived when Blacks migrated there from the Caribbean to work for the U.S. companies exploiting the region's gold, timber, banana, and fish resources.

Dictator Somoza launched propaganda campaigns against communism at the time of the Cuban revolution, and it was from Puerto Cabezas, in the Mosquitia, that the Bay of Pigs invasion of Cuba was launched in 1961. "When the Nicaraguan revolution triumphed, we watched it on TV. It was interesting, but foreign," says Deborah. "There was only air communication between Pacific and Atlantic, and more people got their news from Voice of America than from Radio Sandinista."

Deborah spoke English at school, and Miskito with her mother at home. She had a bike and went to a private school until she rebelled against the protected life her parents had planned for her. She insisted on going to a public school, and there she and ten friends joined the Federation of Revolutionary Students.

"We thought we were great. We painted signs and learned how to use the duplicator and talked to students and even stopped class activities. We thought we were revolutionaries, but we were really just activists, saying words, without knowing what they meant.

"Then in came the Sandinistas. They asked us what we had done. Where were the armed guerrillas? Which leaders had taken to the streets? And when we had nothing to say, they simply rejected us. We didn't rate. We hadn't known state terrorism and we hadn't taken direct action.

"But we had known economic repression and we had known exploitation by the foreign companies, which used our men and our resources and then left us used-up land. We were just not as advanced in our revolution as the Sandinistas.

"They didn't trust us. They sent their own people to organize a revolution for us, but nobody wanted it. It was horrible. We felt totally rejected, and so the people rejected the Sandinistas. They were foreigners. And that is how the trouble started. We were caught between the contras and the Sandinistas, and misled by many leaders.

"It is going to take a lot of education to turn the Atlantic Coast people around, but they have to do their own education, not let it be done for them by Spanish-speaking experts from Managua. I am convinced there is room for all Nicaraguans in the revolution, and that includes others besides guerrilla fighters. The Sandinistas have to trust us."

Part of the trouble in 1979 was that the Sandinistas arrived armed, to confront thousands of Somocista ex-Guardsmen encamped across the Río Coco border with Honduras. The border runs right through Miskito communities and many families had members and land on both sides. Indians made up only thirty per cent of the Atlantic Coast's population. But they had the strongest identity and were the most vulnerable to the contras' counter-revolutionary efforts.

Raiding from Honduras increased and, following a plot to create a separatist state, the Sandinistas decided to move eight thousand Miskito people inland, away from the border. This relocation fired further protests and campaigns organized by the U.S. State Department to discredit the Sandinista government. In 1985 the Sandinistas reversed this policy and began sending the Miskitos back to their original communities.

"Things are getting better now," Deborah maintains. "There is a real understanding of our need for autonomy within Nicaragua." A national commission was created to reach agreements on language rights, land ownership, and education. One of its members is a woman lawyer, Mirna Cunningham, a Miskito woman kidnapped and later released by the contras.

But the ordinary people of Nicaragua, including those of the Atlantic Coast, are united in a more popular fashion by Nicaragua's hit song, an English-language Miskito song called "Banana." When I visited every radio station was playing it. The words were easy to learn:

> All the nations like banana
> Black man like eat banana
> Bluefields like eat banana
> Sumu like eat banana,
> White man like eat banana
> Texas like eat banana.

Sung to a Caribbean beat, the lyrics brought back memories of foreign exploitation as well as feelings of national pride. The banana, from the Atlantic Coast, is a national emblem and something everybody knows.

The band who recorded "Banana" was Saumuk Raya [Miskito for "New Seed"] and it was recorded in jail. When a hundred

Miskitos from Puerto Cabezas were taken to prison in Managua in 1982 for counter-revolutionary activity, they asked for guitars. Comandante Tomás Borge, Minister of Justice, arranged for four guitars to be sent to them, and ten prisoners got together to form the band. They worked all morning and practised every afternoon until they were ready to record, in the Ministry of Culture's studio. In December 1983, all the members of Saumuk Raya got their freedom under an amnesty and began touring the country from the Atlantic Coast to the rest of Nicaragua.

Deborah is a fan of Saumuk Raya, and likes the new magazine for the Atlantic Coast, *Wani*, which is printed in Spanish, English, Miskito, and Suma. She wants to work on a local newspaper when she returns home, but admits that the local press is pretty bad.

"It's very unprofessional, poorly written, badly presented, but there are good things. We have a newspaper called *Sunrise*, that gives people a chance to sound off about local problems, bureaucracy, shortages, waste, and so on.

"We're a noisy, easy-going people. We're more like the Caribbean people than the Spanish in the rest of Nicaragua. We love reggae and Stevie Wonder and jump-ups and sitting around. We have a long way to go to understand the politics of revolution, but we have to go our way. I don't believe my people want to join the contras and many who did go to join them have since realized they were being manipulated.

"We have a saying, that only what you have in your stomach is yours. We will have to wait and see."

Celina

"What is wrong with a dancer shaking her hips and her breasts? They are as much part of her body as her hands and feet, aren't they?"

The girl who challenges me with this is only thirteen. I meet Celina Mendoza at the children's festival of the dance, held in the colonial city of Granada.

Celina dances with a group called Xipaltomal, which performs the traditional dances of the Indian population of Nica-

Celina Mendoza.

ragua, and wins first prize at the festival. They wear grass skirts, fitting tops, headbands, and bare feet. The boys wear nothing but white underpants, and nobody ever laughs, because this is a ceremonial dance, circle-dancing to a drum beat. There are other traditional dances, too. There is colonial dancing from Masaya, where girls wear sequins and feathers and enormous hats with feathers, and flutter their Spanish colonial fans. But I find myself somewhat uncomfortable with the frankly sensual dances of the Afro-Caribbean people of Nicaragua's Atlantic Coast. They call it the Palo Alto style.

Ten-year-old couples shake in a kind of innocent sexual exuberance. They circle each other and shimmy. It isn't the bump and grind of the North American exotic dancer spicing up the happy hour. But it sure isn't folk-dance night at the "Y" either.

These kids are very conscious of their sexual appeal, and they get more applause than anybody else.

I ask the "group mother" for Celina's ensemble to explain the dance to me but, before she can get a word out, Celina speaks up. I am still new to Nicaragua and the articulateness of Sandinista kids surprises me. Celina hasn't just thought about this, she is quite prepared to defend and explain her views on dance and sexuality:

"I'm thirteen. I could get married when I am fifteen. I'm a sexual being, see. We see nothing wrong in a girl shaking her body."

Celina doesn't dance that way herself, because she prefers the ceremonious Indian dances. But she sees nothing wrong with more sexual styles of dance, even when done by ten-year-olds. They are "very Nicaraguan."

I watch again. This time a boy, about ten, half mocking in the role of village stud, chases his reluctant prey. The audience of kids roars encouragement. His performance is followed by a trio of young girls in long red satin skirts. When one girl loses her skirt because it gets trodden on and ripped, she carries on in her briefs without a pause and gets an extra cheer. They all shimmy with the pride of young girls who have just acquired something to shimmy with.

The next dance group is composed of all male break-dancers; another shock for me. They are Michael Jackson clones, moon-walking and spinning, but not very well. Why on earth, I ask, do Nicaraguan children copy the dances of America? Celina has a point of view on this one, too:

"We want to do any type of dancing, and do it better than anybody else. That includes break-dancing. It is a different way to move your body and the boys like it because they get the spotlight. Usually the girls get all the best dances to do. Break-dancing is more fun for the boys."

The show moves on: couples and square dancers, chain dancers and solos, a pair of Spanish flamenco dancers, and a comic dance of old men. Dancing is evidently an eclectic art in Nicaragua. And dancing is just part of the festivities for the Association of Sandinista Children.

Celina was an ANS member long before she began in her dance group a year ago. She likes the traditional dances because they teach her about parts of Nicaragua she does not know:

"When I am dancing like we did today, I feel I *am* an Indian. It is like being part of a dream, and I only wake up when the drum stops and people applaud. Then I feel completely worn out, but happy."

She is also learning to play guitar through the ANS, but she's finding it much harder than it looks. I ask her what else her school group does through the ANS.

"We go on clean-up patrols, around the neighbourhood. We do lots of singing. In a year or so I will be old enough to go on the coffee brigades or take part in militia training, but now we mostly learn about our country and our heroes and traditions, and we have fun like other kids do."

"We children want to laugh and sing" declares the banner over the stage. A boy and a girl from the ANS host the entire show, while two other kids take charge of microphones and music. Other kids are on door control. I look around for adults and find a few mothers arranging costumes, a couple of bus drivers, and one ANS organizer dealing with the press, that's all. Otherwise it is a kids' show, for other kids. Parents can come along, of course, but they would be in the minority. It isn't parents' night at junior high.

I talk to Celina about how Nicaraguan children assume their responsibilities with such ease and how they see themselves and their place in society.

"We're taught that Nicaraguan children never used to have much," she says. "They were sort of left out. Now we want to have fun, to laugh and sing, as we say, but we want much more. We want to be important and to be serious. It would be pretty silly if all we did was laugh and sing when there is so much to be done in our country."

She talks about duties: the duty to learn, to defend one's country, and to help in production by growing vegetables or picking fruit. These are duties to other people as well as to one's self. Celina wants to become a doctor, but, she adds, "not the sort of doctor who gets rich, but the sort who looks after poor people and the children." She knows it will mean a lot of studying, but she believes it is perfectly possible for her to be a doctor, "not like before the Revolution, when a girl didn't stand much of a chance."

Celina is very confident about the future, except that she is worried about the chance of war, fearful of an invasion by the "Yankees."

"We don't believe any children want war, not the children in North America or anywhere. We're suffering now from war. If Nicaragua didn't have to spend money on guns, there would be more money for schools and clinics. We would have musicians for our dance festival and not just tapes. We would have paints and books, all we wanted.

"Children just want to get on with growing up."

She's not against North American culture, either. In fact, she likes a lot of U.S. TV programs, movies, and singers. She's seen the movie *E.T.* She likes Woody Allen. She likes Michael Jackson. She knows a lot of pop songs, and especially likes Olivia Newton-John, Donna Summers, and country and western music. She wants to learn more about the culture of other countries, about China, Japan, and Africa.

"Wouldn't it be great," she says, "if there could be children's festivals that brought children from everywhere in the world to sing and dance together?"

Lidia

You don't become a "queen" in Nicaragua by sucking in your stomach and fluttering your eyelashes. You sweat for it. Lidia Patricia Rivera, the seventeen-year-old coffee queen of Nicaragua, gets up at four a.m. and works until dark, every day, for the three months of the harvest. She picks at the rate of twelve cans a day, four times the average. (I checked, it was true!) With two to three pounds in a can, Lidia brings in $6,000 a season to the Nicaraguan revolution.

I found her on the Asunción Lonisga coffee station, north of Matagalpa, by following the singing. It was impossible to see the army of pickers from the Sandinista Youth, but I could hear them singing and calling to one another, somewhere up the hillside under the glossy leaves of the coffee trees. Lidia is wearing a shallow basket strapped to her waist and a headband to keep the sweat out of her eyes. Her long bangs hang over the band. Although the coffee areas of Nicaragua are comparatively cool,

Lidia Patricia Rivera.

when you work as hard as Lidia you sweat. Her fingers fly along the berry-laden twigs, choosing the ripe, red-tinged berries and stripping them expertly without damaging the twig. This is her fourth year at picking.

"The first year I barely picked one can a day. Then two. I wanted to see how far I could go. It's a matter of practice and having quick fingers, nothing special," she insists. Foreign *brigadistas* who have picked alongside girls like Lidia confessed to me their shame when comparing their meagre results. It is the same in other harvests.

"There's nothing that brings you face to face with reality faster than being out-picked by seven-year-olds," confessed a Canadian volunteer who has worked in Nicaragua's cotton fields.

Lidia, however, comes from a peasant family and has worked in the fields for many years. She has three brothers in the militia. Two other brothers have been killed, one in 1978 and one in 1979. She has done military training, too, and knows how to use a gun, but she doesn't like them.

"I shouldn't say this, but I felt sick every time I squeezed the trigger. I don't like violence."

Lidia was part of the literacy campaign when she was only twelve. She taught twenty-six peasants how to read and write and lived by herself, among them, for six months. The poverty and hunger she saw in the isolated eastern part of Nicaragua led to her ambition to become an economist, "but a practical economist, not somebody who sits all day at a desk."

Lidia seems such a gentle girl. When our conversation shifts to the subject of the contras she becomes visibly upset, remembering their attacks on children. She tells me about a ten-year-old who saw his father and mother kidnapped.

"He followed them for two days, without anything to eat. The counter-revolutionaries wouldn't let him go with his father and mother. They tricked him by saying they would be back in a few hours, so he waited another two days, all alone in the jungle, without food. Eventually he had to go back because there were six other younger children at home, and he had to take care of them.

"He got himself a job at the local store. But he still had responsibility for the family. He had to get the younger kids off to school, and see the little ones were fed. I think it is terrible that children have to lose their parents. It makes me feel hurt, inside."

Last year, when she was picking coffee, the contras came within two kilometres of the coffee fields. And in November, 1984, they burned a plantation close by. Now when they work, Lidia and her work brigade are protected by the militia — a handful of young men and two girls with AK guns and dangling earrings.

The day begins at four-thirty a.m. with a breakfast of tortillas and coffee. Sleepy teenagers eat standing up beside the huge troughs where brown and red coffee beans are soaking. At this time of day, the paths to the plantations are slick with mud, and everything is damp. But the mist soon rises and the birds begin to sing. At lunch time there is rice, beans, and more tortillas. All the kids look forward to "parents' day" when buses bring anxious mothers with cakes. At three p.m., most of the pickers quit, though some, like Lidia, stay until the light fails. At night there are songs and stories by candlelight, but by nine p.m. the huts, each with sixteen wooden bunk beds, are quiet.

It could be just another camp, though primitive by any Western standards. But in Nicaragua, it is a vital pillar of the economy that depends not upon banks and interest but upon small farms, peasant labour, and teenagers like Lidia Rivera.

Diana

Diana Roos, aged twenty-one, spoke up in church. That's what impressed me first about her. We were in St. Mary of the Angels, a circular church built on the ruins of an old one destroyed in the 1972 earthquake. This church, in the poor neighbourhood of El Riguero, Managua, has become the *internacionalistas*'s favourite place for Sunday mass. Murals of Nicaraguans cover the walls: peasants helping Christ with his cross, jungle scenes with parrots and donkeys, women with baskets on their heads. It is a revolutionary art gallery.

But it is the service itself that attracts many people. Father Uriel Molina shares his sermons. He not only encourages the local people to read the scriptures, he sets down his hand-microphone after a short sermon and says, "Now it is your turn. This is your church. You are welcome to come and say what you have in your minds and hearts."

Diana Roos is the first to take the mike. A mane of curly dark hair frames her face. She has a broad smile and bushy eyebrows. Diana speaks up on behalf of the Sandinista Youth. She talks about the threat of invasion, about the fears of young people going into the country to pick coffee where there could be contra attacks, and about their faith in Jesus.

"I believe, very simply, that God protects us when no guns can," she says. "We pray, and we ask you to pray for us."

After reading so many foreign depictions of the Sandinistas as "Communists," I find it fascinating to hear a militant in their youth organization speaking up in church. Diana isn't using the church as a platform, she teaches catechism classes and is a firm Catholic. A large group from the Sandinista Youth help out in religious instruction. She explains:

"It doesn't pose any contradictions at all to us. Nicaragua is a very Catholic country, and it is hardly surprising that many young people are Catholic." There were other, purely Christian, student organizations, but Diana joined the Sandinista Youth because she believes it truly represents young people's desire for change.

There is one church, the "church of the poor," announce posters on the outskirts of Managua. At the Puebla Conference of Bishops in 1979, the church pronounced its "preferential option for the poor." It is this understanding of the role of the church that attracts young people like Diana.

Her father and mother are firm Catholics, and so are the rest of her brothers and sisters. She has been a member of the militia, as her mother has been, for four years. She can handle a gun, and sees nothing contradictory in defending her country and praying for peace.

"I believe that Jesus Christ was a revolutionary in his own way, and that he would be a revolutionary today. All that a revolution means is change. It isn't anything to be frightened of."

Diana works with children in the same poor neighbourhood where St. Mary of the Angels was built and where she was born. She wants to study popular education. She especially likes using puppets in her work, and is interested in learning how to make them and how to create puppet theatre. She wants to get married and have children "just like we all do." She considers herself to be "really a traditional woman. I don't like violence, not even when people shout at each other."

What concerns her most of all is the war the contras have launched. "It is the young who are suffering. We have asked our bishops to protest the kidnapping of eight students who went to the north-east as literacy teachers. They were marched across the border to Honduras by the contras, without shoes and with their hands tied. Early in December, twenty-two young people were shot or burned alive in their bus on the way to harvest coffee. I can't understand how churches in the United States can give money to counter-revolutionaries who burn children alive. Is that Christian?"

Later, I ask Lautaro Sandino, at the Sandinista Youth headquarters, if many members are like Diana.

"Of course. Nicaraguan youth are as diverse as young people anywhere. Just because we have a special duty to pick cotton and coffee and to help in defence doesn't mean we are part of an army. We have the same dreams and needs that all young

Diana Roos.

people have all over the world. Take a look at our magazine, and you will see what I mean."

He handed me a copy, and I found that *Los Muchachos* is full of corny humour. Besides articles on rock and roll and art, the magazine publishes pen pal names and addresses and the words of the latest hit song, "Banana." There is an exercise program to get rid of a spare tire, illustrated with amusing cartoons, indicating that even Sandinista youth get fat and lazy. I was fascinated to see it even published a sex column, rated number-one reading by the youngsters I spoke to.

Nicaragua has no program for sex education in the schools, except for biological references to sexual organs. According to *Los Muchachos*, the war against Somoza and the following literacy campaign plunged many young people into a freedom they did not know how to handle. There were kids who were used to rigidly supervised family settings. The sex column is there to help young people develop their own new morality on sexual activity. Many young people I spoke with thought their parents were sometimes still living in the past. Lautaro gives me an example of a mother arriving at military headquarters at three in the morning to demand if her daughter was all right!

"Parents need to understand that our children are not like those of Costa Rica or Venezuela or any other country where they have to ask permission to go to the movies, or to come home late. Young Nicaraguans know how to act and speak for themselves, they can spend six months in the country and think nothing of it. They can handle weapons. They cannot be treated like babies."

But the teenagers themselves also need advice in how to care for each other and how to prepare for their own families. They still believe that "The family is the basis of the new society and we have to create this family with a sense of responsibility."

The Sandinista Youth stresses the active participation of its members in the new society of Nicaragua as their main duty. This means participation in sports, education, and culture as well as in production and defence. What they saw as the main problems facing young people in Nicaragua struck me as being quite similar to those facing North American youth: unemployment and relationships with parents and partners. But Nicaraguan youth also confront scarcity and the pressures of war.

Lautaro Sandino is not sure how many of the forty thousand Sandinista Youth members are Catholic. He says only that "Those who are Catholic are some of the very best." At St. Mary of the Angels, Diana's church, it was a bunch of students from the congregation who, in 1971, created their own Christian community. They organized help after the 1972 earthquake and then helped the community get a better water supply, a health clinic, and decent roads. The popular movement that spread from Christian-based communities like theirs brought them into the Sandinista front and active work against the Somoza army.

"I don't really think about the split between the Archbishop's church — what we call the church of the salon — and the church of the poor," says Diana, when I ask her about the growing divisions.

"If I don't know what to do, I ask myself what Jesus would have done. And I don't find any difficulty in deciding what that would be, and what I must do. It is really very simple."

Martín

Martín Henríquez is twelve years old. He has no idea why he is in a school for "high risk children" in Matagalpa, in the heart of Nicaragua's coffee-growing region. He lives with his grandmother, who is "very good" to him.

"She lets me do anything I want," he boasts to me. "I can stay out until three o'clock in the morning if I want to."

"And that's why you're here," replies his teacher.

Martín is one of some thirty children who have been sent to this special school because they are believed to be in need of protection. Some of them are shoeshine boys or work part-time in the market. Some sell newspapers. A lot of them are children whose fathers have either died or disappeared. Some drop in and out of school. A few, but very few, are thieves. Some have no warm clothes. All of them need more attention than most kids do, and they get it in this special school.

The school expects them not only to do as well as other kids, but also to do better. Pinned prominently on the school wall is a message from Commandante Humberto Ortega, recalling that Carlos Fonseca, who was a key early revolutionary in Nicaragua, also sold raffle tickets and newspapers as a kid:

"Out of the poor, humble Nicaraguans like this, in the fifties and sixties, came the forces that changed our history."

The special schools are run by the Social Security and Welfare Institute. Their programs have two main purposes: to protect children at "high risk" and to help those who were falling behind in schoolwork, two problems that are usually interconnected.

In spite of the revolution, in all Nicaraguan cities there are still droves of kids eking a living by selling candies and fruit, toys and newspapers, fireworks and cigarettes. Most of them, it is true, wear shoes and look in much better health than the child beggars of Honduras, Guatemala, or El Salvador. But they are nevertheless a problem. They should be in school, preparing for the future. The Sandinistas view these children's problems as economic and cultural. Many Nicaraguans who grew up illiterate never valued education for their children. Rather, they considered it was their right, as parents, to profit from their children's work.

Besides these working children, there are the kids whose parents have been displaced by the war with the contras, those who have lost fathers or mothers, and those who simply got lost in the shuffle of families. There are also some who were delinquents, though there are remarkably few of these.

Martín isn't a serious delinquent, just "undisciplined." His father was killed by the contras three years ago. Martín says he cannot remember him. His mother works in a chicken factory in Managua, but he hasn't seen her for a long time. Another brother and sister live in Managua, but he does not know where.

"I am head of the family because I am the eldest man," he announces proudly. His grandmother has admitted that she has trouble controlling him, and local teachers reported he was hardly ever in school, but always running around the streets at night.

"When he did attend class, he was very bright. But he was also very adventurous, the sort who could easily be led into bad ways. He could have turned out really bad, so we brought him into our special school," explains his teacher, Adelis.

Now Martín spends all day at the school. Some other kids come just for the morning or the afternoon, because it is recognized that many have to carry on with their jobs to support themselves or their families. They all go home at night. Their parents are encouraged to attend regular meetings so they can learn what the school is doing, and give their own suggestions.

"We never treat their parents as stupid. Sometimes they are much more intelligent about their children than any outsider, however qualified in psychology. We are not taking their children away or making them feel they are failures as parents. We simply want to give extra encouragement."

Martín and his fellow students were given their own toothbrushes at the school. For some of them this was the first time they'd possessed one. They have regular academic classes, and extra enrichment classes in music, arts, and crafts. They learn woodworking and electrical repair. Once, the kids even repaired an old electric fridge. They are given a big lunch. Martín says he's just eaten a lunch of meat, onions, rice, and oranges.

"My old school was very noisy. We had forty kids in our class, and the kids tore up the school books. We had lots of games, but I didn't learn very much," Martín says. "Here we have one teacher for every ten of us. We are going to have a garden and grow vegetables. We play baseball. We go on trips. We are going to the city of Estelí very soon. I like school, now."

Martín wants to be a mechanic. He loves cars and wants to learn more about electricity so he can install lights at home. He also enjoys reading and his favourite book is the dictionary.

"Tell me a word, so I can look it up," he begs me. "I do that, and then I copy the word down. I like the sound of them, as well as the meanings. I like big words; words like constitution and revolution." He also likes stories about heroes and adventures. At home there is no TV, but sometimes he watches it at a friend's house. His favourite programs are Superman and stories of the Nicaraguan revolution.

Martín is typical of most of the kids, though more articulate than some of the others. Some, especially the girls, are very shy. Children in the younger class are making straw horses, rabbits, and clowns. There are never enough paints for everybody, though these classes are given special supplies. There is also a clinic to help those with health or learning problems, such as dyslexia.

"Nearly all these kids are a couple of grades behind, though they do not lack intelligence," explains Adelis. "They lack concentration. It is hard for them to sit still. Part of the problem is that they live in a fast, adult world when they are working, and it is not easy for them to sit down quietly and study. They are not really mature enough for work, but they are forced to help out financially. Very few of them keep any of the money they make. Very often they feel a tremendous sense of responsibility to help out, and are worried sick if they lose a few pennies or get robbed by the gangs who sometimes prey on newspaper kids or shoeshine boys.

"Very few of the kids here are totally without family or homes. I've only known one little girl like that; she slept under a tree, before we found her a proper home. They usually have shoes, too, though not very good shoes. Their jackets aren't thick enough for the cold up here, so we have a clothing store."

A Nicaraguan government survey of some four thousand working children out of the two hundred thousand children in Managua between ages seven and fifteen showed that very few earn money by begging. Very few smoke marijuana or drink beer, though the researchers admitted the children might not be telling the truth. Certainly, it seemed to me that drugs were not nearly the problem in Nicaragua that they were in Honduras. A lot of these kids live only with their mother because the father has "disappeared." If their parents work in the market, that is where the kids work, too. It is much safer for the kids if their parents work close by. The kids who sell newspapers, pop, or balloons, on their own, are more likely to be prey for thieves or to be roughed up by bigger kids.

One big difference between the street kids of Honduras and those of Nicaragua is that the kids in Managua can read and write. Many of them go to school part-time as well as work. True, they began school later than most kids, and not all are doing well, but they do have some schooling.

Most kids work six hours a day, but some work as many as twelve. The Sandinistas would like to establish workplaces that offer some protection for those children who have to work. But, given the many economic problems of Nicaragua, that won't happen just yet. In the meantime, Martín and his fellow students are getting a good education and somebody to care about their progress and behaviour.

What difference will this make to a kid like Martín?

Institute experts frankly do not know. It is hard for them to evaluate the importance of all the resources and challenges facing these kids. Children such as Martín still have to cope with the upheavals and dislocations caused by the war, as well as with economic hard times. Yet they are also affected by the new spirit of co-operation, enthusiasm, and desire for progress the revolution has created.

Santiago Duarte.

Martín Henríquez.

Santiago

Not all young Nicaraguans love the Sandinistas. Santiago Duarte doesn't, for one. He is secretary-general of the youth organization of the Independent Liberal Party (PLI), which ran against the Sandinista National Liberation Front (FSLN) in the November 1984 elections. They won eight seats (the FSLN got sixty-nine and the Conservatives thirteen). We meet in the PLI headquarters, in the basement, where the tables are marked out for chess. Santiago is very self-possessed; a good student from a good family. Though his politics and attitudes remind me of junior politicians, Western-style, his articulateness and enthusiasm are typical of young Nicaraguans.

"You see, we are not monsters. We hated Somoza and fought against his regime just as much as the Sandinistas did. All we want is an option. We are the people who fought for freedom, and we want our freedom now that the revolution is won," he declares, almost as soon as we sit down.

Santiago grew up as the only son of a business family, living in Granada, one of the most conservative and traditional Nicaraguan cities. He was barely affected by the revolution.

"We hardly saw any fighting. We knew the revolution had triumphed when all the church bells began to ring. It was something we watched on TV," Santiago tells me. "We weren't touched at all." He continued at school, a private school, when he moved to Managua and, like his father before him, joined the Liberal Party. He is just seventeen, the age when he has to register for national service, and that bothers him a lot.

"Why do the young people have to die? Why doesn't the regular Nicaraguan army take care of the contras? It isn't fair. I suppose I would fight, if the Sandinistas would give me a choice; I don't like being forced into it, though.

"Nicaraguans are like that. We're all rebels at heart. We won't act if we are forced into something. They should ask us first."

Santiago does have a choice — to leave the country, because he has family in the United States. But he wants to stay. He thinks he may very well register for the army after all, because he doesn't want to be thought of as non-revolutionary.

"That is the trouble. We are forced into a situation where

you either have to be Sandinista or you are seen as the enemy."

Santiago has no intentions of picking coffee, either. He has no desire to join the thousands of young Nicaraguans who work in the production brigades. He knows that "where the kids are" there is a lot of danger, and he has heard they get political indoctrination and lectures every night. He thinks this is wrong. He really wants to be a businessman. For now, he sees his duty as studying and argues that study is the best way for youth to serve their country.

He insists it is not true that the Liberal Party opposes military service or advises young people not to register. The party merely informs young men what their rights are.

"We have boys coming to us all the time asking how they can get out of the army. Most of them are from families who work in the market, or else their fathers are businessmen. Their families need them."

Santiago worked during the November 1984 elections, giving talks in schools "when we were allowed in." Most of his talks were to students in the private schools. "It was threatening, having to talk to the kids in the public schools. They simply did not want to hear us."

He cannot give me any actual instances of intimidation. It was more a feeling that nobody was listening. It was quite different in his own private school. He estimates that at his school there were only five hundred members of the Young Sandinistas out of a student body of two thousand.

"We don't carry arms or anything, but it is obvious that the Sandinistas think of us as the enemy. There are students who report our behaviour to the FSLN. There is not the reality of pluralism that the Sandinistas claim. When you try to give opposing views on history in the class, it is impossible to express yourself because the other students won't let you. And I know there are spies."

Santiago thinks the FSLN has never really tried to seek peace with the United States, but is trying to antagonize the White House, thereby threatening his country. He wants a more conciliatory foreign policy. But he makes it clear he would fight for his country if the United States attacked. He insists that the Liberal Party fought against Somoza just as hard as the Sandinistas, though he did not know anyone in the Party who had been killed, tortured, imprisoned, or wounded by the Somoza army. Santiago sounds very defensive for much of the interview, but, to be fair, his attitude is the stance that most Western kids would take if submerged in a revolution.

"I agree that Somoza was evil, but the path of revolution has been strewn with thorns. There are shortages of toothpaste. There are no buses. Food runs out in the stores. There is always this pressure to defend the country, to pick coffee or cotton, to do what you are told, by those who don't represent me — they only represent one sector of the people."

At the beginning of the revolution, he was much less critical. He felt a sort of "euphoria." Everybody was happy. "I felt it too in my heart and there was hope for everybody. The young people did community work but they did it without being told to. The times were critical. Now, a lot of that enthusiasm has evaporated, but they are still bugging us to work when we should be studying. We have a right to fulfil our potential as individuals."

Santiago hates guns and doesn't know how to handle one. He does not like the idea of Nicaragua being militarized, and he thinks the housewives training with rifles on Sunday mornings look "ridiculous."

"Let's be fair," he challenges me. "How would you feel in Canada if you were told you had to spend all your spare time running around with guns? I bet you would not go. So why should you criticize us if we take the same attitude? If this country were governed better, there would be no need for tanks in the streets, and grandmothers at target practice, and children picking coffee when they should be in school."

Santiago reads the opposition newspaper *La Prensa*, but no other newspaper. He hasn't heard about a recent attack by the contras on a busload of young coffee-pickers. He doesn't dispute that three thousand children have been killed by contras since 1982.

"I don't approve of anything done by the counter-revolutionaries. They are bad men. I just disapprove of the way we are being forced into a war, when it should have been possible to avoid it," he explains. "I am all for peace. And I believe Nicaraguans are a pacific people, too."

About his own, personal future, he isn't too sure. A lot depends on the advice his father will give him on whether to stay in Nicaragua or get a "better" education in the United States. Maybe he will be a politician, but probably he will be a businessman, like his father.

"All I want is to have that choice, to stay or go, to fight or study, to pick a career, to say what I want and think as I want. That's all."

Freddy

I literally bumped into Freddy, or he bumped into me, when the wheelchair brigade from ORD (Nicaragua's Organization of the Revolutionary Disabled) rounded the corner as I was running for a bus.

Freddy Trejos is a wheelchair revolutionary, one of the founders of ORD. When he was nineteen, a bullet in the back severed his spinal column. He was trying to save a couple of kids caught out in the streets by the sudden arrival of Somoza's National Guard. He managed to push them to safety in an open doorway and then he was shot.

For three days he lay bleeding on the steps, unable to move, feeling his lungs collapse and his eyesight fade. Then his *compañeros* came to his rescue.

"If there is one good thing I learned from that experience, it was that your friends do not let you down. Nobody is alone," Freddy says. In 1980 he helped found the ORD. Now there are six hundred members, all disabled, mostly from the war that ended Somoza's dictatorship. They counsel, instruct, and help find work for ten thousand other disabled people.

Their wheelchairs are made from bicycle wheels. This is the Nicaraguan special model, which costs $300 instead of $1,000 for an imported chair. Friends from the United States bring in the wheels and the frame is put together from aluminum tubing. All the work is done in the ORD workshop, which both services and employs the disabled.

Wherever I go, I keep on bumping into the wheelchair revolutionaries — at religious celebrations for the Immaculate Conception and at demonstrations outside the U.S. consulate protesting the kidnapping of Nicaraguan students by the contras on the Honduran border. Freddy and company are even planning to help in the coffee harvest, if they can only find somewhere flat enough to manoeuvre their wheelchairs.

"We feel we have a special duty to be in the vanguard. If we are there, then there is no excuse for others to stay home." Up to now, he has been very serious, very dignified, but suddenly he grins.

"Okay, it is propaganda in its effect on the people, I admit, but it is important for us. If we don't want to be thought of as victims, we have to prove we are leaders. We have to prove it to ourselves as well as to others."

Freddy was born in Masaya, to a peasant family. He joined the Sandinistas when he was only thirteen. At first, it was more of a learning experience than active militancy. He worked in a sugar factory. From 1977 until he was hit by that bullet, he was with the guerrillas.

"It was terrible when I came out of hospital," he admits. "I lost contact with the Sandinistas because they were so busy and the country was in tremendous disorder. I felt tremendously despondent, being unable to take part in building the revolution. But then the FSLN became concerned about the hundreds of wounded fighters. Some of us were sent to hospitals outside the country, to Cuba, for example, where we learned how to take care of ourselves and got back our dignity as human beings. And when we returned, we organized the ORD."

Freddy and his fellow disabled Sandinistas took the name of Ernesto Che Guevara as the symbol for their organization, because Che, too, was disabled.

"He had asthma so badly he had to have oxygen. But that never stopped him. It only made him determined to do more than ordinary people. If he could be like that, then he should be our inspiration."

ORD members work in the regular world as electronic technicians, mechanics, draftsmen, and political organizers. Freddy welcomes the computer age, which makes the man in the wheelchair just as good as anybody else.

"You won't find us weaving baskets and making brooms," he says. "We're not helpless victims who can just manage a few simple crafts. We're as good as anybody else. That is why we have the motto: *Todos podemos* — all of us can."

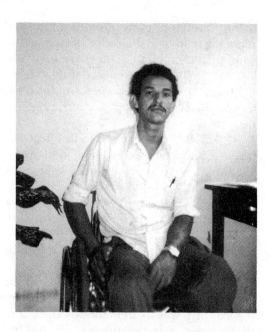

Freddy Trejos.

Freddy is now twenty-four. He is married, with one son, and has travelled to Canada and Costa Rica to take part in games of the disabled. Sports is a big part of the ORD program, especially basketball, weight lifting, and wheelchair races.

While I am talking to him, some other ORD members are taking English classes, others are working in the shop, repairing chairs, and another group is painting a storehouse to make more live-in accommodation. They have an old van with lifts for wheelchairs, but it doesn't have a windscreen and nobody knows when the spare part will arrive. The lack of medical equipment and spare parts for chairs and walking devices really hinders the ORD.

"There is so much to do. We are now working with polio victims and the blind, not just those disabled from the war."

Polio has now been eradicated in Nicaragua; there has been no reported case in two years. Now the older victims of the disease, once hidden away, are coming forward. There are disabled children, too. A UNICEF program, administered through the Nicaraguan Ministry of Health and the Ministry of Education, sends "promoters" into the towns and villages. The promoters are themselves mostly teenagers. They collaborate with the ORD to provide exercises and encouragement to kids who have been kept at home in ignorance and shame.

Freddy thinks that all the disabled should have access to ORD programs. There is even a disabled former member of Somoza's National Guard working with them — clearly, past bitternesses are forgotten.

Freddy doesn't want me to give the impression that everything is going well, however. He is very conscious that enormous problems still face the disabled in Nicaragua.

"Try finding a taxi! Just try! They don't want to be bothered with a wheelchair. I've waited hours and given up, many a time. That's why we've all got these big muscles, see, pushing ourselves along, up and down the hills. We have to cope with curbs and steps and pot-holes and places where it is simply impossible to get into a building in a wheelchair. Ways of thinking change slowly, and some people still think of us as helpless. Even worse, they are embarrassed by us. We remind them of the war. We make them feel guilty. And now, there are the new disabled, the kids injured in attacks by the contras. We have to help them get over the emotional shock, and then the difficulties of living."

Their task seems enormous, but Freddy and company don't seem tense or exhausted by the difficulties. The house in a sidestreet that is their office and repair shop is cheerfully disordered, and filled with local visitors. Everybody seems to know the ORD.

When I get back to my hotel, a middle-aged American, a carpenter, talks to me about his daily run-in with the Nicaraguan bureaucracy that is thwarting his search for volunteer work. He can only stay another week and isn't in shape to pick cotton. I send him to see Freddy. The next evening he arrives home late, with paint all over his pants and an enormous smile on his face.

"I told him I wanted to do some work. He didn't understand my Spanish, so I drew a picture. He asked me if I could paint, and got me a brush and there I was all day, painting the storeroom and mending chairs. They'll let me work there tomorrow, too."

Angelita

Angelita, from El Salvador, and her best friend, Rosario, from Nicaragua, are hanging side by side from the monkey bars. To find a kids' gym at a refugee camp is surprising in itself; to find a seven-year-old Salvadorean refugee playing with a girl from her host country is even more unusual. But then, this is not like the other refugee settlements I have seen in the rest of Central America. This, I am reminded, is not a "camp" at all, it is a co-operative.

Some twenty-two thousand Salvadoreans have found refuge in Nicaragua, more than those in the much-disputed camps in Honduras. The co-operative I visited, twenty miles north of Managua, is large. It has seventy acres under intensive cultivation — watermelons, corn, peas, tomatoes, beans, and a thousand hens (soon to be increased to five thousand when some new buildings are built).

The big difference between this and other refugee camps I notice immediately is the lack of barbed wire or guards. There isn't even a gate. Salvadoreans can go wherever they want. There are barely twenty-five people there during my visit, the rest are in town or "visiting."

There are kids on the slides and swings, kids running around in the hay. I keep getting confused, discovering half of them aren't Salvadorean refugees at all, but Nicaraguan neighbours.

"What are you here for?" I ask one Nicaraguan boy.

"To get eggs," he replies smartly. But he's been here since lunchtime, and is in no hurry to leave.

"The local people are always coming over, especially the kids," explains Tiburcio Vigil, the spokesperson for the co-operative. "Sometimes I'm not sure myself who is a refugee, and I'm supposed to be the person in charge."

Angelita has been in the co-operative two years. She says she can't remember El Salvador, and has been best friends with Rosario "for always." They play together every day. Angelita and the other kids go to school under the big tree, beside the slides. Rosario goes to school two miles down the road, but she comes to play as soon as school is over. Sometimes Angelita goes to her house.

"She gave me this hair ribbon, see? We do everything together," explains Angelita.

The co-operative has its problems. Medical supplies don't always come, and sometimes the doctor who is supposed to come once a week doesn't arrive either, so they have to take sick children to a neighbouring clinic. They aren't quite self-sufficient in food yet. They get some help from the United Nations refugee organization, mainly in the form of tools. But they are free to sell their produce as they want, and to buy what they need.

"We're in charge of our own affairs. It's still not the same as living in your own country, but we feel we are with friends, and that makes a lot of difference," says Tiburcio. The Nicaraguan government has given them seeds and a plough and has also arranged bank financing for the chicken project. "They are not our bosses. They give us advice, and if we are stupid, we ignore it. We've come to trust them."

That is why some of the younger men and women from the co-operative are going to pick coffee with the Nicaraguan brigades. Six hundred Salvadorean refugees make up a special brigade. It is their way, they explain, to say thank you to the Nicaraguans who have given them shelter.

In a 1982 report, the World Council of Churches described Nicaragua's reception and integration of Salvadorean refugees as "exceptional":

"Unlike all other Central American states, Nicaragua does not regard the reception of refugees as a burden or a danger but as a real and concrete way of showing its solidarity with brothers of neighbouring countries."

CONCLUSION

FLYING HOME, safe, to my own children and grandchildren, I could not get the children of Central America out of my head. They live so close to the edge. I started to think of them as the children of the volcanoes that dot the Central American landscape and are part of the local folklore — beloved but unreliable gods. Like the societies of Central America, volcanoes can lie dormant for years and then erupt violently, showering down death, in a wave of destruction that cannot be stopped. Yet the volcano is the people's friend: its ashes fertilize the barren earth and help new life to grow in abundance. The children I met were both part of that violence, and part of the promise of new life.

They had already enriched me with a new understanding, and I began to think a great deal about what we can do to help them. Should we bring them north for adoption? Sponsor individual children in their own countries? Send money for community projects? Rely on the church to take care of the problems? Support governments only if they take better care of their own children? Or try to help oust the regimes so that a more humane government can tackle the problem?

Not even development agencies agree which option is best. But with so much to be done, any help is better than indifference, so it is well to examine every option.

Adopting kids is a deceptively attractive person-to-person

aid. Surely, with so many childless couples in North America, it would be better for a Central American kid to grow up North American — with all the material advantages that entails? But most Central Americans condemn such foreign adoptions as child-stealing. They believe it is denying a child his or her own birthright; they equate it with genocide. By material standards, maybe, an orphan would be better living with a North American family than in a Central American refugee camp, but the local people do not feel this way. They do not think only of material matters and are highly suspicious of the rich couples who pay up to $12,000 for a child, encouraging a local black market in babies.

It is also important to remember that children without mothers and fathers are not considered abandoned, because they are part of an extended family. And how can anybody be sure the mother and father are dead? They could be lost in the shuffle of refugees around Central America, or they could be fighting in the hills and will come to claim their child as soon as they are able.

Child sponsorship used to be considered the best solution, but the practice has run into criticism in the last few years. One child may benefit greatly, but the aid often stops with that particular child, very often isolating the recipient from his or her less fortunate brothers, sisters, and friends, and encouraging envy and materialism. It also means that social workers spend their whole time translating "thank you" letters into English for North American sponsors who rain inappropriate gifts like ice skates and video games on kids in need of pencils and shoes. Thousands of sponsors have eased their guilt and acquired "new families" through sponsorships, but the results for the children and their societies are debatable.

Many development agencies have turned, instead, to village or program sponsorships, which involve aid of a more tangible benefit to the many. A well, a clinic, a vegetable garden, or a chicken co-operative can affect a whole community for the better, and also encourage the people to take part in their own development, instead of being always a charity case. Community sponsorship has also taken over from some of the children's homes established by foreigners, places that removed kids from the community. But what to do about the several million displaced people, most of them women and children? Any project that relieves the misery of refugee camps can save the children. In Central America the people are not indifferent to the plight of children, though the rich and, too often, the governments turn their heads away. They see the problem as a lack of financing and are reluctant to risk encouraging self-development, especially when this involves helping people educate and organize themselves. Aiding local groups has to be done with extreme sensitivity to local conditions. Well-meaning aid can so easily draw the attention of reactionary regimes. The American nuns murdered by the Salvadorean army are not an isolated example of the danger of actively participating in community aid programs within a delicate political situation. And local workers run much higher risks.

The Catholic churches may, or may not, be vitally important in helping the hungry, depending on whether or not they follow the teaching that the Church has a special duty to help the poor. Evangelical Protestant sects are much less likely to be rooted in the community and are often seen as outsiders, bringing in a foreign religion. Too often, they combine preaching the Word of God with extolling the values of a capitalist society.

Pressuring a reactionary government to change its ways or forfeit aid has not proved very useful. Instead, it has led to a charade of body counts; statistics paraded in order to persuade foreign governments that human rights violations are down, and to convince them to resume aid suspended because of documented atrocities. Certainly, repressive regimes that do get official bilateral aid from other governments treat such help as a sign of respectability and use it to justify continued oppression.

Development agencies face a dilemma. If they stay in a country, however repressive its regime, they can find themselves used. If *they* can take care of the kids, why should the government do so? And if *they* continue to work in a country, that surely indicates it is not an international outcast. If an agency cannot accept these conditions and pulls out, it leaves behind the people who need it most.

In the long term, the only solution for Central America's children must rest with the people of Central America. If they can be helped, but not directed, towards changing their societies, the children will be the first ones to benefit. In Nicaragua, for example, the first national project after the 1979 revolution was a literacy campaign. And it was followed by health programs.

No children's program is possible, however, if countries have to cope with war. And war includes the threat of intervention, foreign militarization, and the iron fists of military regimes and dictators. Anything that contributes to the bringing of peace to Central America will benefit the children in a much more profound way than Christmas gifts. But, as any mother or father knows, it is much easier to buy off a child with toys than to answer the child's real needs.

Many times, I wondered how Central American kids could watch TV commercials — usually with their noses pressed against the store window — that mirrored North American opulence without hating the people who dangle such images of delight in their pinched faces. But they do not hate. Even in Nicaragua, amid banners demanding "Yankee Go Home — *Fuera Los Yanquis*," kids still preserve an image of the North American as basically kind, generous, clever, and lucky, not really responsible for the excesses and abuses perpetrated by government.

I gave my flashlight to a ten-year-old boy who ran messages for the FMLN fighters in El Salvador. He unhooked the tiny bead necklace around his neck, made for him by his sister, and insisted I take it.

Maybe we should think more about what we can learn from such kids, and less of what we think we can teach or offer them.